W9-ALM-527

ALLie'S
AnSWeRS

**Other Books in
The Seekers Novel Series**

Holden's Heart
Rebecca's Return

Available Spring 2002

Ben's Big Break
Tess's Touchstone
Frank's Fear

The Seekers Novel Series

ALLiE'S ANSWERS

by

G. J. Linko

J
LIN

Allie's Answers
by G. J. Linko

Editors: Jeffrey S. Nelson, Ronald Klug, Carolyn Berge
Cover art: Chris Wold Dyrud
Cover design: David Meyer
Interior design: Carolyn Berge

Scripture quotations are from New Revised Standard Version
Bible, copyright © 1989 Division of Christian Education of
the National Council of the Churches of Christ in the United
States of America. Used by permission.

Copyright © 2001 G. J. Linko. All rights reserved. Except for
brief quotations in critical articles or reviews, no part of this
book may be reproduced in any manner without prior written
permission of the publishers. Write to: Permissions, Augsburg
Fortress, Box 1209, Minneapolis, MN 55440-1209.

ISBN 0-8066-4179-7

Manufactured in U.S.A.

05   04   03   02   01   1   2   3   4   5

Augsburg Fortress

5.99

For Greg.
You are my best friend
and my inspiration.
Thank you.

1

NOT HOMEWORK!

I looked around at the other members of the Seekers youth group sitting in a circle of folding chairs. Swinging my ponytail over my shoulder, I began telling the story of my most embarrassing moment: "When I was in second grade, I was jumping rope at recess."

Rebecca and Tess began to giggle. They had heard this before. The rest of the kids stared at me intently. "I had dressed myself that morning in one of my favorite outfits: red and white striped T-shirt and my favorite wraparound jean skirt."

I pretended like I was dressing myself, just to ham it up a little. Holden let out a burst of laughter. He'd been there when this had actually happened. "Excuse me, Mr. Cross," I said to him sarcastically and put my hands on my hips. "You may save your reaction until I am finished."

"No problem, boss," he said laughing. He gave me a playful salute, signaling me to go on with the story.

I resumed where I had left off. "Anyway, for you boys who don't know what a wraparound skirt is, it's a skirt that just ties around you. No elastic or buttons or anything to hold it up. Being the fashion plate that I was, I decided not to double-knot the skirt, because that would look too dorky. So, I just tied it once. And as I was jumping rope at recess, my skirt fell completely off, showing off my beautiful blue-flowered underwear for the whole school to see!"

The circle of kids roared in laughter as I took a triumphant bow and then sat back down. I looked over at Rebecca and Tess. They were giggling along with the others.

"But, wait, wait, " Holden was stifling his laughter. "There's more." He stood up to finish the story.

"Hey, this is *my* most embarrassing moment, Holden. You think you could keep from horning in on my story?" I reached over and gave him a playful shove. I knew he wouldn't let me get away without telling the "kicker" at the end. He continued as if he hadn't heard me. I covered my face with my hands and pretended to be embarrassed. Actually, I liked the attention.

"Anyway, folks," began Holden dramatically. "Allie's skirt is lying on the playground. All the kids are just dead quiet. Everybody's staring at her, like waiting to see what she's going to do. Nobody's even laughing. And Allie, she looks over at her friends twirling the rope—her skirt still lying on the ground—and she says, 'Well, don't just stand there, do something!' And she looks at them like it's their fault!"

All the kids sitting in the circle collapsed in laughter again, holding their sides. Holden sat down and looked over at me victoriously, pushing his brown hair out of his bright, blue eyes. I smiled at him and laughed. What a geek I had been in second grade!

Our youth leader, Miranda, was fresh out of college with lots of long, curly, red hair and a friendly smile. While everyone recovered from the story, she got up from her chair and went to the middle of the circle. It was time for our youth meeting to end, and Miranda was about to give her end-of-the-night talk.

She began, "Allie, I don't know what was more entertaining, the story itself or the thought that you actually wore a skirt!" More chuckles around the room. She was right. That was pretty funny. Did I mention that I'm a tomboy?

Miranda went on, "I want to say thank you to all of our open-mike participants. I think it's important for you guys to talk to each other openly and get to know each other better. It makes our group a lot more fun, and tonight's stories of embarrassing moments were particularly hilarious. I'm sorry we don't have time for more, but I need to explain your homework for next time."

At the mention of the word "homework," the entire group groaned. You couldn't say that word to a group of junior high kids and expect to get a good reaction—especially in the summer.

"I know, I know," Miranda said. "But this won't be too much work, and you might even have a little fun!"

We quit moaning and listened. All of the kids in the Seekers youth group here at the Christian Community Center like Miranda. She has a lot of energy and tons of great ideas, and she really likes us kids. So, I think that most of us didn't even mind when she asked us to write a prayer journal for homework. She told us simply to write our prayers down on paper. That way, we would be more inclined to really think about our prayers, take the time actually to pray, and organize our thoughts. She promised she wouldn't read them. These journals were only between God and ourselves. *I wish God would write us back*, I thought to myself, only half joking.

"Now, just because I'm telling you I won't read them, doesn't mean you don't have to do them," Miranda said, waving a scolding finger at us. She knows how the junior high mind works. "I will check to see that you have them next week. So, please bring them with you next Tuesday. Oh, and another thing: Remember we have an extra meeting this week on Thursday— same time. We have to go over some last-minute details for the dance on Friday and the festival on Saturday."

These were the biggest events of the summer here in Golden Oaks for us kids. We wouldn't forget.

"Any questions?" Miranda asked, as she turned in a circle to look at all of us. "Okay, guys, I'll see you on Thursday. God bless."

As I walked out of the community center with my friends, the street lights were already turning on. After an afternoon thunderstorm, everything smelled fresh and alive. A half-crescent moon was shining in the sky, its light reflected in the puddles on the sidewalk. Lightning bugs flitted around in the town square. It was a perfect summer night. My friends and I started for home.

"Well, Allie, you sure know how to tell a great story," said Rebecca, one of my best friends. She twirled a finger around a piece of her short black hair.

"Like you haven't heard that story a thousand times."

"Somehow it gets funnier every time," said Holden.

Rebecca and Holden slapped each other five, and Tess laughed quietly.

"Don't make me start reminiscing about your extremely eventful childhood, Holden," I teased. "You know I can tell stories about you."

"Well, you already told all of Mrs. Jenkin's social studies class last year about my toadstool trick! What could be worse than that?"

"I've got worse stories than that about you, Holden. You don't live next door to someone for 13 years and forget to keep some dirt on them." I smiled mischievously. "You never know when it might come in handy."

"Is that right?" he teased.

"Yeah, Holden," Rebecca chimed in. "Next week at Seekers you're going to have to give us a story."

"You know, Allie, you sure are brave to get up and talk about your most embarrassing moment like that," said Tess. "I could never say anything up in front of a group!"

Tess is really quiet and reserved. Despite her shyness, she became one of our best friends soon after she moved to Golden Oaks last fall.

I answered, "Aw, you could do...." I was interrupted by the soft swoosh of bikes coming toward us from behind.

We all whirled around to see who it was. Before we could react, the bikes flew full-speed into a puddle on the street, splashing all of us with cold, murky rainwater. We could hear the two bike riders laughing maliciously as they rode away.

"Jerks!" Rebecca yelled after them, wiping the rainwater out of her eyes. "Look, my new shirt is totally ruined," she wailed.

Tess and I stared at the muddy stains on Rebecca's neon-pink shirt.

"That was Trent Gage and Chris Hawthorne," said Holden, shaking his head and looking after them. "One of these times...." He let his voice trail off, fists clenched at his sides.

"I can't believe them," I said. "The nerve!"

"Doesn't surprise me," said Tess under her breath, wringing out her long, dark brown hair. "Doesn't surprise me at all."

I saw Holden throw her a questioning glance, but he said nothing.

Chris and Trent are notorious troublemakers in Golden Oaks. They are a year older than the rest of us, and they are the meanest eighth graders I have ever known. They're always doing some crazy prank. Last year, the rumor was that they scared away every substitute teacher in the whole school district. The principal himself had to act as the substitute for a few days, because he couldn't get anyone else to do it!

We walked for a block or so in silence. There wasn't much more to say about those two. The best thing we could do was steer clear of them.

We reached the corner where we had to go our separate ways, the corner of Grand Boulevard and Pinegrove.

"I'm off," Tess said, taking off down Grand.

Rebecca turned the opposite way from Holden and me on Pinegrove. "See ya," she called.

"Not if I see you first!" I returned, smiling.

"So, are you going to write your prayer journal tonight,

Allie?" asked Holden as he stopped to tie one of his gym shoes.

"Yeah, I probably will. Except, well, there's...there's one thing that's bothering me about that," I said.

"What is it, Al?" asked Holden, as we started walking again.

"Well, it's just that in church and at Seekers, everyone tells us to pray and everything. Don't get me wrong, I really like to pray. I always feel better when I do. But, well, they always talk about how God answers us. I just don't know how that works. How does God answer us?" I looked over at Holden to see whether he knew what I meant.

"Haven't you ever gotten something that you prayed for, like an A on a test or something?" Holden asked.

"Well, sure," I said, "but I mean even more than that. How do we know what God wants us to do? Stuff like that," I said, knowing that I was having trouble making my point. "I don't know."

"I know what you mean. It's like you hear people like Pastor Bob at church talking about how he knew God wanted him to do this or that, like God helps him make decisions." Holden glanced at me to see if he was on the right track.

"Yeah, exactly," I said, glad that he understood. He's good at understanding.

"I know. It is weird. I'm not sure what Pastor Bob means either. Ask Miranda. She'll be able to give you a better answer than I can, but I do think that God answers us. Maybe we just don't know where to look."

We'd reached Holden's house and were standing under the glow of the streetlight. "Yeah, you're right," I said. I wanted to talk more but I knew that it was time to check in with my mom.

I started to turn toward my house, and then I remembered one more thing. "Hey, where was Ben tonight?"

"He couldn't come. It was his brother's birthday. We'll have to explain the homework to him."

"Yeah," I said, "and tell him how he missed my most-embarrassing-moment story."

"Oh, yeah." Holden grinned. "And how he missed our mud bath, courtesy of Chris and Trent."

We said good-bye, and I walked slowly down the sidewalk to my porch. The big yellow two-story house looked inviting, but I decided to sit on my porch in the rocking chair and enjoy the night air for just a minute. As I rocked, I thought about the dance and the festival coming up. It was going to be fantastic. Every year, the town square would fill with booths for the craft show and food, as well as a carnival, a stage for different bands and shows, and tons of other fun stuff. It was a kid's dream, and the dance on Friday night was strictly for junior high kids. It was held in the community center gym. Not only was there dancing, but food, games, and contests. At this time of year in Golden Oaks there just seemed to be a buzz in the air.

I giggled to myself, remembering how last year Holden and I had spent almost $10 trying to win this ugly green unicorn thing for me at the milk-bottle toss.

The porch light suddenly turned on. "Mom, you scared me!"

"Sorry, Allie. Didn't mean to." My mom opened up the door, walked over to the porch swing and sat down. "Pretty night, isn't it?"

I nodded.

"Did you have fun at Seekers tonight, honey?"

My mom is a totally cool mom. She's like my friend too. I told her about the meeting and we sat there for a while, talking about the festival.

"We'd better go in," she said finally. "I have to get up early and work on some things for the high school float in the parade." My mom teaches at the high school. The whole town was gearing up for the big weekend.

I kissed Mom good-night and I went upstairs to my room to get ready for bed. I pulled on my favorite T-shirt and boxers that serve as my pajamas, and then I struggled with my first prayer-journal entry. It took me a while. I wasn't sure whether I was doing it right, but I did get it done. As I dozed off to sleep, I thought about the festival. It was going to be a great weekend!

2

TESS'S TEARS

The next morning, I got up and read over the journal entry that I had written.

Dear God,

> *Thanks for our youth group, Seekers. We all have a lot of fun being in it. We learn a lot and do cool things. Thanks also for what a big hit my story was at Seekers tonight! One thing I wanted to ask you, though, is to help me figure out how you answer our prayers. Help me to listen for those answers. Also, by the way, if you want to help me with my jump shot, that would be fine too. I mean, next year I'm going to be in eighth grade. How am I supposed to play basketball without an awesome jump shot?*
>
> *Thanks for the festival and the dance too. It's always so much fun!*
>
> *Please bless my mom, me, and my friends.*
>
> *Love, Allie Johansen*

It was short and sort of…well, blah. I wanted it to be deep and inspired. I wanted it to be profound and important, but I figured this was really what I was thinking about, so I guess it was what I should pray about. I decided that when I asked Miranda about how God answers us, I would also ask her whether my journal was okay. Or maybe I would just ask Rebecca. I wanted to know whether I was doing it right. I mean, when you put your prayers in writing, it makes you see how silly some of the things are that you think about—like a jump shot. Shouldn't I have prayed for world peace or help for the homeless?

I stashed my journal under my pillow and got dressed to go jogging. I slipped on a pair of running shorts and a tank top. I automatically brushed my long, sandy-blond hair into a ponytail—my signature style. My legs were feeling a little tight, so I stretched them out a little. I tied on my running shoes and bounded down the stairs and through the kitchen.

My mom waved as she took a gulp of coffee.

I yelled, "Morning, Mom," as I went out the back door. She is used to my jogging in the morning. I have been doing it for three months, getting ready for basketball season. I love to keep myself in shape.

Running clears my head, gives me time to think. I set out on my usual route up to the junior high schoolyard, around the track, and back home. It was a beautiful morning with the birds singing and the sun shining. It was already hot and beginning to feel steamy again, even after last night's storm. As I ran, I thought about what a fun summer I was having and all the cool things we would do this weekend at the festival. As I turned down Pinegrove toward home, I spotted Holden shooting hoops in his driveway.

When I got close enough, I called, "Well, if it isn't Michael Jordan! Want to play some one-on-one? Or don't you want to get beaten by a girl again?"

Holden looked up with a defiant smile. "Sure, let's go, Allie. I've been working on my jumper. First person to 10 wins, as always." He passed me the ball and the game began.

Holden has lived next door to me forever. We have been good friends since we were about two years old. I can remember when we both had training wheels on our bikes. (I got mine off first!)

The score was tied 8-8 when we took a break to get a drink out of the hose. As I started to take the hose from Holden, a mischievous grin broke out across his tan face, and there was a sinister twinkle in his blue eyes. He was putting his thumb over the waterspout.

"Don't you even think about it!" I yelled, just as the first drops of water sprayed me right in the face.

Holden and I struggled for control of the hose—the ultimate summer weapon—both of us becoming completely soaked. We both finally gave up because we were laughing so hard.

"You knew you couldn't beat me, so…so…you figured you'd try revenge—revenge by hose!" I gasped. I sat on the edge of the deck to wring out my ponytail.

Holden snorted. "You had no chance in the game, just like you had no chance against the hose, Alliecakes." He used the nickname my parents used for me when I was little, because he knows how much it annoys me. He took off his T-shirt and put it over the back of one of the lawn chairs to dry in the sun.

"Very funny, Cross." I noticed Holden must have been working out—getting ready for cross-country season. Holden is tall, lanky, and strong looking. He looks like an athlete—a typical runner. Still, he's no match for me on the basketball court, even though he is a couple inches taller.

"Well, let's go finish the game, Alliecakes." Holden shook his head over me so the water in his hair would drip on me.

I got up to accept the challenge when, out of the corner of my eye, I caught Rebecca walking down the sidewalk toward my house. She didn't even notice us because she was listening to her portable disc player.

"Hey, Rebecca, wake up!" I yelled at her from the deck. She didn't even flinch.

Holden put two fingers in his mouth and whistled. That did the trick.

Rebecca turned abruptly and saw us. She smiled and strolled over. "Well, if it isn't the Picasso and Rembrandt of the athletic world." Rebecca's mom is an artist, and Rebecca loves drawing, sculpting, and especially painting.

"I'm surprised you noticed us, space case," I teased.

"Hey, I have an excuse this time. Mom and I were up late sitting on the roof of the apartment building, looking at constellations. Boy, the sky was clear last night. What happened to you guys?" she asked, noticing we were sopping wet.

"Nothing. We just got carried away getting a drink of water," I said. Holden and I looked at each other and laughed. "Did you cut your hair again?" I asked Rebecca, absentmindedly dribbling the basketball through my legs.

Holden walked by and swiped it from me. "Or did you just

get into a fight with the scissors?" asked Holden and went in for a jump shot. He loved to kid Rebecca about how her look changed every other day.

"Yeah, ha ha, Holden," Rebecca replied. She ran her hand through her short, tousled hair. "I liked my pixie haircut, but I thought it needed to be more messy looking. So, I just chopped it up a little bit. You like?" she asked, batting her long eyelashes and taking a few exaggerated steps as if she were a runway model.

"Yeah, looks just like the magazines," I answered. "You did your makeup different too. And, hey, cool dress! Girl, you are looking good." She had on a yellow dress with a huge 1970s collar—very retro, but she could pull it off. Her eye shadow was glittery and she had on frosty pink lipstick. She was quite a trendsetter, and all the boys at school flipped for her.

"Yeah, thanks, Allie. I see you got some new summer clothes too—new running shorts and a tank top." Rebecca sighed as if she'd given up on me. She had been trying to get me to grow some fashion sense and wear makeup since the sixth grade, when I first met her.

"Hey, I've got to be practical. I couldn't beat Holden in basketball if I was wearing high heels and a skirt!" I clutched my heart, exaggerating.

Rebecca giggled. She and I sat down on the lawn chairs on the deck. I turned mine to face the sun. Holden went on shooting baskets.

"The only makeup I need is a suntan, Rebecca," I said.

"Ugh, wrinkles. That's all I've got to say," Rebecca said as she pulled a pair of bright green, cat-eye sunglasses from her backpack. Rebecca carried her clear, plastic backpack everywhere. It was always stocked with everything that made her Rebecca: makeup, sketch pads, disc player. Rebecca sat up straight in her chair and put her sunglasses at the end of her nose, looking over them. She stared at Holden shooting hoops and said, without taking her eyes off of him, "Look at that. He is a cutie, Allie."

"Who? Holden?" I said. "What are you talking about? It's Holden, Rebecca." I stared at her in disbelief, but she was still watching him. "I guess I've known him too long. Or maybe, hey, maybe you are just boy crazy, as usual." I took her sunglasses from her and put them on.

Holden came up to the deck and put on his shirt. I never could understand how Rebecca could think he was so cute. I mean, I guess he is good-looking, but he's my friend. I don't know. I've just never thought of him that way.

Holden looked at both of us. "Are you done with the girl talk? Is it safe for me to come back?"

"Calm down," I said. "Hey, can we get something to drink?"

"Sure," answered Holden, "I was just about to get some lemonade. You want some too, Rebecca?"

"No way. Thanks, though. I'm on a health-food kick. No liquid sugar."

Rebecca's always doing something weird. "So did you write your journal yet?" I asked her, hoping she'd give me some idea if I did it right.

"Yes, I wrote it under the stars last night. I just wrote about some things I was thankful for. Oh—and I asked God to help Tess's grandma to get better."

"I forgot about that," I exclaimed. Tess's grandma lived with Tess and her family. She is a great lady. Before she got sick, she used to make the best food for all of us—wacky stuff like peanut-butter-and-banana sandwiches and pineapple-ham pizza. It sounds gross but it's awesome. We loved that stuff. And we loved her stories. She always had a smile on her face and some fascinating tale about her adventures as a kid. Some bordered on the unbelievable, but we never cared. It was just so fun to listen. Tess really loved her "G-ma," as she called her. Her grandma's sickness was really hard on the whole family.

"I'm going to have to put that in my journal too," I said. "How is G-ma doing?"

Holden had returned with the drinks and handed me mine. He jumped into the conversation. "My mom saw Tess's mom at the grocery store. She said G-ma's not doing too well." We sat in silence for a minute. We didn't want to hear that news.

"I wrote about the festival in my journal, you guys," I offered, hoping to get everyone's minds off G-ma.

"I can't wait until the weekend," Rebecca said. "Think about how much fun it always is. This year, I am going to win a gold-fish. These are my goals: win a goldfish and dance with at least 20 boys!" She rolled her eyes in exaggeration. We all laughed, even though we knew that if Rebecca wanted to, she could.

Holden took a drink of his lemonade and said, "I can't wait to ride the new roller coaster that everyone is talking about."

I nodded, "Yeah, I should put that in my journal too. Please, God, don't let me barf my guts out when I ride the roller coaster with Holden."

Holden groaned. "By all means, God, take care of that."

Rebecca looked at Holden. "Hey, what did you write about in your journal?"

Holden looked a little surprised, caught off guard. His cheeks became a bright red for only an instant, and, for some reason, he glanced quickly over at me. "Uh...nothing really. I...uh...."

Just then Tess came tearing down the driveway on her mountain bike. Her long, brown hair was tangled from the wind. She looked upset. She stopped, letting her bike drop carelessly on the ground.

We stood up, looking at each other, bewildered.

Tess ran onto the deck, out of breath. She was normally so quiet and put together, but now, her large, greyish-brown eyes were filling with tears behind her glasses.

I couldn't wait for her to catch her breath. "What? What happened? Is it G-ma?" I grabbed her arm and led her to one of the lawn chairs.

Tess sat down, looking around like she wasn't quite sure what was going on. She began, "No, G-ma is fine, fine. I, uh...."

"What? What?" Rebecca practically yelled. We were getting scared. This wasn't like Tess.

"G-ma's fine," continued Tess, searching for the right words. "I was on my way out of the library this morning." Tess volunteered at the library each morning in the summer, and when she wasn't there volunteering, you could often find her there reading. "And I saw this sign taped to the handlebars of my bicycle." It was the first time that I noticed she was holding a folded piece of white paper in her hand.

"What? What does it say?" asked Holden, clenching his jaw.

Tess handed him the paper.

Rebecca asked, "What is it? A love note?" She was trying to lighten up the situation. But as Holden unfolded the sign and held it up so we could read the two words scrawled in black ink, we knew that this was nothing to make light of. Tess put her hand over her face to hide her tears. The rest of us gasped in a mixture of fear, surprise, and anger as Holden crumpled up the horrible sheet of paper that read "CRIPPLED DORK!"

Rebecca immediately ran to Tess and crouched next to her chair, trying to talk to her and calm her down. Tess was crying hard. Rebecca grabbed Tess's right hand—her good hand—and I could see that it was trembling.

Tess had been in a car accident when she was little, like four or five, I think. As a result, her left arm hung limply at her side. Tess could barely move it, and then only when she concentrated hard. She was so good at doing everything one-handed, you forgot that she had this disability. She swam, rode bikes, even played basketball. The thought of that sign on her bike was horrible—no, worse than horrible. It was the meanest thing I had ever heard.

Holden pounded his fist on the wall of the house and began pacing back and forth. "I'm sure we all know who did this!" he half yelled.

I nodded, knowing that he must be thinking about Chris and Trent just like I was. "Yeah, who do they think they are? Let's go find them. I want to tell them what I think of them!"

Holden and I got up to leave.

Tess looked up at us, wiping her eyes. "That won't help, you two."

There was something in the way she said it, something quiet yet forceful that made Holden and me sit back down. Even though every bone in my body wanted to find those kids and let them have it, I didn't want to go against Tess.

Rebecca turned to us, looking very serious, and said, "You need to calm down. Tess needs friends right now, not hit men. You don't even know for sure it was Chris and Trent. And you know you'll only be asking for trouble if you go see them."

I looked away, feeling a little ashamed. I knew deep down she was right, but I was just so mad!

Holden spoke my own thoughts when he said, "I know you're right, Rebecca, but Tess shouldn't have to put up with that. Those kids need to learn a lesson and...."

Tess cut Holden off. She calmly said, "Holden, I haven't been able to use my left arm for nine years. I've had to put up with a lot of staring, mean remarks, and rudeness. Some people act like they don't want to touch me or get too close because they think it'll rub off." She paused and wiped away a tear. "I've learned to ignore a lot of it, but it hurts. And this," she said, pointing at the crumpled sheet of paper now lying on the deck. "This...I just never thought...." Her voice trailed off. "Please don't go after anyone. Don't make any more trouble. I'll be fine in a few minutes." She started to cry again softly.

We sat there silently for a minute. My mind was racing, not believing what had happened. I said softly to Tess, "You should tell your mom and dad. They'll help you."

Tess shook her head. "No, not now. Not while G-ma's sick. I don't want to give them anything else to worry about. I'll be fine."

"But, Tess," I pleaded, "you should tell them, or we could tell my mom."

"No, Allie, not now. Promise me you guys will just forget about this. Just forget it. I was just a little upset. I had to tell someone, but it's over. I'm fine. Promise me you won't tell anyone." Tess looked at us, her teary eyes pleading. She tried to smile.

Holden, Rebecca, and I looked at each other. I knew she wasn't fine. I could tell by the looks on their faces that they didn't think she was fine either. But what could we do?

Rebecca looked thoughtfully at Tess and said, "It's our secret, if that's what you want, Tess." Rebecca glanced at Holden and me.

"Yeah," I said, "if that's what you want. We're your friends."

Holden looked at Tess, shook his head, and said, "I guess, if that's what you want."

Tess smiled gratefully. I hugged her, feeling unsure whether forgetting about this incident was the right thing to do. The worried expression on Holden's face told me he had doubts too.

Rebecca, trying to change the subject and brighten the mood, jumped up and said, "Let's all go get ice cream and forget all of this."

"It's not even noon yet," Holden said.

"So what?" I piped up. "Let's live a little. It's summer!"

Tess quickly agreed, glad to have something new to focus on. Holden picked up the basketball to put it in the garage and said, "Hey, Johansen, the score is eight to eight. Don't think I'm going to let you off the hook."

"We'll finish it later," I called as I ran to my house to tell my mom where we were going. *I have something much more serious to write about in my prayer journal now*, I thought. I wished that my jump shot was still my biggest worry. *Are we doing the right thing forgetting about this? Will they keep terrorizing Tess? What should we do?* More than ever, I wished that it was possible for God to write me back.

3

WHat SHould
WE DO?

Tess, Rebecca, Holden, and I walked lazily toward the town square, licking our ice-cream cones and trying to remember the words to the Golden Oaks Mustangs' victory song, for some reason. In the square, the park benches and picnic tables were nestled cozily between gardens of petunias, snapdragons, and lilac bushes. The great oak trees formed a shady canopy, offering relief from the hot summer sun. There were little kids running around, their mothers chatting with each other on the nearest benches. We saw kids from our school just hanging out.

We found an empty bench and sat down to finish our ice cream. Watching as the first of the festival booths were being set up across the square, we talked about anything and everything—except the one thing we were all thinking about.

"Hey, there's Ben," said Tess, pointing toward the clock tower. Sure enough, Ben was dribbling a soccer ball toward us, waving wildly. I laughed under my breath. Ben is the last of our awesome friend group. He is a terrific guy—a riot, sort of like a class clown. When he's around, you just can't help laughing. He is shorter than me, with dark hair that sticks out in a billion different directions and glasses that never sit quite straight on his nose. He was obviously coming from soccer practice, but even now, he had his camera around his neck. He's the photographer for the school paper.

"Hey, ladies and germs," he yelled when he got close enough. "How's it going, guys?" He was smiling broadly and dribbling the soccer ball.

"What's up, Benny?" I said. "Missed you last night."

Holden leaped and kicked the soccer ball away from Ben. "Yeah, I told him all about Seekers," Holden said.

"Wish I could have heard your story, Allie. But it was funny enough when Holden told it to me." As Ben stuck his tongue out at me, I gave him a playful swat. Ben looked around at Rebecca and Tess still finishing their ice cream. "What? None for me?"

"You can have the rest of mine," Tess offered quietly, barely looking up at Ben.

"Thanks, Tess, but I was just joking." He took out his camera and took a quick picture of Tess. He smiled. "Sorry. Couldn't resist. You have a little ice cream on the tip of your nose." He took the napkin from Tess and wiped it off. Tess giggled, flushing with embarrassment.

Rebecca looked at me and winked. She never quits. Always trying to set people up.

"No, really, you can have my ice cream if you want it, Ben," Tess offered again.

"Hey, no problem. Thanks," Ben grabbed the cone. "Now I

need my picture taken too." Ben started chomping messily on the ice cream until it was all over his face. Then to our delight, he plopped the cone upside-down on top of his head. "Cheese!" he yelled, handing his camera to Tess. We were laughing hysterically as Tess clicked the picture.

Holden sprinted up from where he had been kicking the ball around. "Hey, what's with the ice cream, Benny?"

"What ice cream?" Ben asked, deadpanned, as a drip of butter-pecan fell into his left eye.

This started a whole new round of giggles from us girls. Holden shook his head, chuckling.

"Ben, you're a nut."

"Yes, a pecan to be exact. Butter pecan," Ben said between laughs.

This was what summer was supposed to be like. All of us goofing around in the square, laughing and having fun. Still, Tess's note from this morning hung like a thundercloud above us—a thundercloud that nobody wanted to talk about.

Ben started going crazy, taking pictures of everyone. We were used to it. Ben had documented practically our whole lives on film. Rebecca struck a thousand different poses as usual. She could never resist a camera. She was sucking her cheeks in to look like a movie star and cracking us all up.

"Take one of Allie and me," said Holden. He ran toward me and draped his arm around my shoulders. *Oh, brother*, I thought, *I can already hear Rebecca's comments about this.*

"I need to talk to you," Holden whispered in my ear.

"What about?" I whispered back. The serious tone to his voice made me very curious and a little nervous.

"Tess," he said. "We need to talk about that whole thing."

I nodded. "Yes, we do. But not in front of her. Did you tell Benny?"

Holden shook his head. "I'm going to go off and play soccer with him now. I'll tell him all about it. Find a way to come over by us." He pulled on my ponytail and ran off with the ball, calling for Ben to follow him. Out of earshot of us girls, they were kicking the ball around, but I could tell by the serious looks on their faces that Holden was giving him the lowdown on everything that happened this morning.

I sat down on the ground by the bench that Rebecca and Tess were sitting on. They were already giggling.

"What was Holden whispering about, Allie?" Rebecca asked coyly. "Did he profess his love?" Rebecca and Tess gave each other five.

"Stop it, you guys," I said, laughing. "You're ridiculous."

"Oh, Allie, take it as a compliment," Tess said. "You know, he really is such a nice guy. You should feel lucky, not embarrassed. Even if you don't feel the same way about him. It's still flattering."

"Allie does feel the same for him, Tess," Rebecca chimed in. "She's just too stubborn to see it."

I was looking over at Holden and Ben, trying to think of a way to get over there so I could hear what Holden had to say, without making Tess and Rebecca suspicious.

"Look," said Rebecca, "she can't even have a conversation with us. She's too busy looking at Holden!"

"Oh, stop it!" I scolded. "Give it a rest. I don't like him. He's my friend, okay? Just like he is yours."

"Oh yeah, just like Ben is just Tess's friend," Rebecca chided.

Tess turned a shade of scarlet and giggled.

"Ladies," I said, "I'm going to leave you to your romantic dreams." I stood up to leave and brushed the dirt off my shorts.

Tess said, "Don't be mad, Allie. We're just kidding. And, hey, Rebecca's just jealous because, for once, the hottest guy in Golden Oaks isn't in love with her."

"Yeah, who'd have thought that gym shoes and skates could win out over makeup and a cool wardrobe," Rebecca laughed.

"Very funny, guys." I trotted off toward Holden and Ben. I didn't know what I was more happy about, getting to hear what Holden had to say, or getting away from their teasing. I was glad that Tess and Rebecca were in such high spirits. Rebecca is good at that. She knows how to keep your mind off of the stuff that's bugging you. I knew that she and Tess would sit and talk about boys and school, and Rebecca would never give Tess a chance to think about this morning. I joined Holden and Ben in kicking the soccer ball around.

"Allie, I can't believe that note on Tess's bike this morning," Ben said through clenched teeth. "It makes me furious. It has to be Chris and Trent." He shook his head. "Why do they have to pick on Tess? They can pick on me. I don't care. But why Tess?"

"Chris Hawthorne and Trent Gage are mean," Holden answered. "They just like to put other people down to make themselves feel good, but we can't let 'em get away with it."

"Were they the ones who gave you such a hard time about being in the musical last spring, Benny?" I asked.

"Yeah, and when I joined chorus in the fall. But they were never this mean, or maybe it just seems so much worse 'cause it's Tess." Ben shook his head. "She's just so...."

Holden looked at me as if to say, "We've got to do something." We kept kicking the soccer ball back and forth, more out of frustration than anything.

Ben continued, "You guys remember last year when Chris and Trent kept knocking my books all over the ground and tripping me and stuff?" Holden and I nodded our heads. "Well, you know that when that was going on, Tess baked me cookies one day and left them in my locker. Now, what kind of person could be mean to someone like that, to someone who would take the time and make cookies for a geek like me?"

Holden looked at me, then Ben. "You know it has to be Chris and Trent who did this to her. We've got to do something. Let's just go talk to these guys. Tell them off."

The more we talked, the madder I was getting, so I agreed. "Let's go. Let's see what they have to say for themselves."

Ben looked at us and shook his head. "Sorry, guys. You'll have to do that on your own. I'm not going to set myself up for an all-out war with those two. I don't think you guys should either, because they won't retaliate with just words. You know that. You're just mad. Give yourself some time. You'll get over it, and we'll talk Tess into telling her parents or something, or maybe we could tell...."

"Tess doesn't want us to tell anyone," I reminded him.

Holden's cheeks were flushed with impatience. "I can't just sit here. I've got to do something."

I looked at Holden and said, "I hate having to just sit here and think about it happening again too, Holden. But maybe Ben is right. I mean, I *know* he's right deep down. It's just hard to see that when we care about Tess so much and we're so mad. Let's just wait for a while." I put my hand on his shoulder and looked into his eyes. "You know Ben's right. We'd be asking for trouble."

Holden shook his head and looked down. "I don't want to let them get away with this. But I know it too. I just feel so helpless."

Ben looked at both of us. "Here come Tess and Rebecca. We better shut up about this. You guys are doing the right thing. Trust me." Then louder, so they could hear, he yelled, "Play ball!" and kicked the ball toward Tess.

That afternoon we tried to forget about the morning's problems. We hung out in the square, eating hot dogs for lunch, playing soccer, and inventing a new game that Ben coined "Seekersball." We even got Rebecca to join in. Occasionally, I'd catch Holden looking at me. I could tell the conversation with Benny was still bothering him. It was bothering me too. The little voice in my head kept telling me that Ben was right, but why did the rest of me want to knock some sense into those troublemakers? I decided I'd write in my prayer journal about it.

The hot afternoon sun slanted lower, and our shadows became visible on the freshly cut green lawn. The clock tower chimed five times, time to get going home for dinner. Rebecca was coming with me to spend the night, so she walked down Pinegrove with Holden and me.

The three of us walked in silence in the late afternoon air, Chris and Trent still very much on our minds. When we got to

Holden's sidewalk, he trotted up his steps. I yelled, "See ya."

"Not if I see you first," he responded, smiling.

Rebecca and I climbed the steps to my house and went inside. My mom had just started dinner. We helped her make spaghetti, and it was delicious. After dinner, Rebecca and I painted our toenails—a different color for each toe—while we watched a couple of classic horror movies. That was a tradition with us. We always rented horror movies when we spent the night at each other's houses. We popped popcorn and put lots of butter on it, and just scared ourselves silly. "Best friends fright fest," we called it.

After the movies we stayed up late talking. We talked about the usual—boys, the festival, how eighth grade would be a blast. Rebecca and I could talk forever. It was 1:30 A.M. when I looked at the clock above the TV. "We'd better go upstairs and get ready to go to sleep," I said yawning. We got up, stretched, and dragged ourselves up to my room.

Rebecca began, "You know, Allie, I saw you and Holden talking today and...."

"Don't even start with that stuff!" I was too tired to get into that.

"No, no, I don't mean how he likes you, Al. I mean, I could tell he was probably still thinking about going after Chris and Trent." Rebecca looked at me intently.

I couldn't lie to her. "Yes, he was, but Ben talked him out of it. I have to tell you, Rebecca, there's a big part of me that wants to say Holden is right." I looked at her to see how she would react. I felt guilty, but it was true.

"I know, I know. Me too, Allie," she said. I must have looked surprised. "Don't look at me like it's so unbelievable, Al. I get angry too. You just can't let that run your life."

"I know you're right, Rebecca. Just sometimes...." I looked away.

"Promise me you won't do anything, Al."

"Okay. I know you're right, Rebecca, deep down."

We got into bed and turned out the light. Rebecca was asleep in no time. But I had a million thoughts running around in my head. I crept quietly out of bed and grabbed my journal. I tiptoed into the bathroom and wrote my second prayer-journal entry. This time I wasn't worried about how silly I sounded or what I should pray about. I was just worried about Tess. And worried about what we should do. I sat for a while as the questions float-ed through my head. *Should we tell my mom? What will they do next to Tess? Is it wrong to want to defend her?* I was tired and feeling a little lost, but I wrote my entry anyway. I knew I'd feel better if I did.

> *Dear God,*
> *I know you know all about this situation with Tess.*
> *First of all, help these bullies to stop. And help us*
> *to do what's right. What should we do?*
> *Allie*

4

Don't Do It, Allie

I woke up to the sound of the phone ringing at the frightful hour of 8:00 A.M. I answered the phone, trying to sound as awake as I could. "Hello?"

"Hi, Allie." It was Tess. Her voice sounded shaky and scared. "It's happened again."

"What?" I screamed into the phone.

"Can you and Rebecca come over right away?"

I thought I could hear her stifling her crying. "We're on our way." I hung up the phone and began changing.

Rebecca, awake by now, had heard my end of the conversation.

"It's happened again," I told her. "That's all she said."

Rebecca looked worried. "We'd better get over there," she replied.

We got ready as fast as we could. We ran downstairs and yelled to my mom that we were meeting Tess for breakfast. She gave me a suspicious look, but didn't press for any details. I was glad. I wondered how long I would be able to keep this from her—or how long I'd want to.

We jogged the four blocks to Tess's house. When we knocked on the door to the large brick two-story house, Tess's mom, a pretty woman in a long white dress, answered. She was leading Tess's little twin brothers by the hands out the door. The boys looked excited.

"Hello, young ladies. Nice to see you again," she said with a smile that looked a lot like Tess's. "I'm taking these two rugrats to the park. They need to be outside. Help yourself to breakfast on the table. There are bagels and cereal." She opened the door to the minivan in the driveway. It was obvious that Tess hadn't told her mom about the situation.

"Thanks, Mrs. Cole," Rebecca and I said in unison, eager to get in and talk to Tess.

As Mrs. Cole was putting the boys in their car seats, she called to us, "Ladies, G-ma is upstairs sleeping, so if you don't mind, keep your voices low. Thanks!"

"Of course," I answered softly.

"Will do," chimed Rebecca.

We ran inside and up the stairs. When we got to Tess's room, we knocked on the door. Tess opened it, looking scared and frail. Her mouth was drawn tight.

"Tess, what is going on?" Rebecca asked. Rebecca and I sat down on Tess's big, fluffy bed with the white canopy. Tess was folding her pajamas quickly and efficiently using her one arm and her chin. She is amazing. It made me think of the time she beat Ben in basketball.

"Guys," Tess began, her eyes tearing up. "Read my e-mail."

She pointed to the computer sitting on her desk. I sat down at the desk and wiggled the mouse to get the screensaver off the screen. Then, I saw it.

Tess,

> *One-armed freaks are not welcome at the festival*
> *this weekend. Just thought you should know.*

I gasped out loud. Rebecca came over and read the e-mail message over my shoulder. I deleted the offensive message in one angry stroke of the keyboard. I didn't want to look at it. I didn't want Tess to have to look at it ever again.

"Why did you do that? Now we can't see who it was from, Allie," Rebecca said.

"Oh, like we don't know," I said, fuming. I was pacing back and forth now.

"I didn't recognize the e-mail address anyway," Tess said.

Rebecca ran over and gave Tess a hug. "Forget about that stupid note. Whoever is doing that is an idiot."

"Yeah," I said. "Forget about it, Tess." Even though I knew I couldn't. "You don't deserve this, Tess." My voice was rising. "This is RIDICULOUS!"

"Shh. G-ma is sleeping next door," said Tess.

"Oops, sorry. I know she's not doing well, Tess." I looked her in the eye. "But I think that you should tell your parents about this. You wouldn't be bothering them. They want to be there for you, Tess." Tess looked away. She was crying again. I glanced at Rebecca. She looked worried.

"I can't tell them, you guys," Tess said. "G-ma's getting worse, and my parents were up all night caring for her and my little brothers. I can't do this to them."

"We're not going to tell if you don't want us to, but I agree with Allie," said Rebecca.

"I know, but…I just can't do it now. I just needed to tell you about it. That's all. I'm fine. I am. Really. It's just hard to take on your own, you know?" Tess went to her mirror and started to brush her long brown hair. She took a tube of lip gloss off her dresser and put some on her lips. I watched her open the lip gloss one-handed, and I was reminded of how capable she is.

Tess turned to us and said, "Let's go downstairs and get some breakfast." She started down the stairs, and Rebecca and I followed. On the way down, I gave Rebecca a nudge with my elbow. Rebecca gave me a glance that said, "What should we do?" I raised my eyebrows in indecision. Rebecca shrugged and shook her head. I didn't think Tess could be fine all of a sudden, no matter what she told us.

While Rebecca and I munched on bagels, Tess whipped us up a mushroom omelette in minutes, using one hand to cook better than I could with two.

"Y'know, Tess, you're a great cook," I said between mouthfuls. "How'd you learn it?"

"G-ma taught me. She says I'm a natural. Of course, I had to work extra hard because I only have one good hand," she said proudly.

I smiled. "I know," I said, "and I admire you." At that moment, it was hard not to get angry all over again about Tess's e-mail message, but I kept my cool for Tess's sake.

"You know, Tess," Rebecca began thoughtfully, "one thing we could all do is write about this stuff in our prayer journals.

We could ask God what to do."

I nodded in agreement.

"I've already done that," Tess answered. "You're right. It does help. I've been praying about it ever since I got the first ones...." She stopped as if she had said something she hadn't mean to.

"First ones?" I asked. "What do you mean? Wasn't yesterday's note the first one?" I glanced from Rebecca to Tess. Rebecca looked as astonished as I felt.

Tess began to busy herself with cleaning up the kitchen. She struggled for words. "Nothing, guys. I didn't mean...."

I could feel the anger welling up inside me. *Were there more nasty letters, more threats? How long had Tess been keeping this to herself?*

"How long has this been going on, Tess?" I practically yelled.

Tess was crying. She wiped her eyes and sat down in one of the kitchen chairs. "Ever since we moved here last fall." She took a deep breath, like a great weight had been taken off her shoulders, and she began to sob uncontrollably. Rebecca ran and knelt next to her, holding her hand. "But, now," she continued in between sobs, "they are...more...frequent. I've been hiding...it because I was ashamed. And now...now...I can't tell because of G-ma. And it is those...those...two boys. I know it." She covered her face with her hand and cried.

Rebecca put her arm around her and looked up at me, questioningly.

"That's it! That's all I can take," I said as calmly as possible. "I'm going to take care of this, Tess. Don't you worry." Inside, I was seething. My face was flushed and I could feel my heart pounding. I ran for the front door.

Rebecca yelled after me, "Don't do it, Allie! You'll regret it!"

I ran out of Tess's house. I was angry and irrational. I wanted revenge.

5

WHAT HAVE
WE DONE?

I ran as fast as I could. All I could think about was confronting Chris and Trent. *I can't believe this has been going on so long*, I thought. I was furious with those boys. They had hurt Tess for something she couldn't even help. It wasn't fair. I kept running. I had to get to Holden's. He would understand how mad I was. We had to do something. I had prayed for answers. Where were they? Chris and Trent had done something wrong, right? So they deserved to get told off, right? And if they decided to turn it into a fight, well, then, fine! I realized hot tears of anger were running down my face. I wiped them on my shirt and kept going. I was almost there. I didn't want to think about this anymore. Enough thinking.

I could see Holden coming out of his house. I watched as he took off jogging up the street, away from me.

"Holden, wait! Wait up!" I screamed, out of breath. He heard me, waved, and began jogging in place to wait for me.

"Hurry up, Johansen. I have the Olympics to train for," he

yelled, laughing.

As I got closer to him, he could see my face. I was sweating, and my eyes were red from crying. I ran up to him and bent over with my hands on my knees to catch my breath.

"What is it, Allie?" he asked. He sounded worried, almost frantic. "It's Tess again, isn't it? I knew this wasn't over."

I looked up and nodded gravely.

He looked right into my eyes. "I knew it. Wait till I find those idiots!" He was pacing back and forth, growing more angry with each step.

"There's more." I had finally caught my breath. I quickly explained how Tess had been receiving horrible notes since she moved here last year, how she knew who it was, and why she hadn't wanted to tell. With each detail, Holden's jaw dropped a little farther.

"Holden, I know that yesterday you wanted to find out who it was and go after them. But do you think it's right? What do...."

He cut me off. "Of course. They have been doing this for close to a year. We need to put them in their place. We have to stop them. Do you think it's fair what they're doing to Tess? I know you don't. Now, if Tess won't let us tell anyone, then we have to handle it ourselves. She is our friend. We have to do this for her, protect her. If getting in a fight is what ends up happening, then fine. But we have got to go find Chris and Trent and get them to stop one way or another." He looked at me, waiting for my response.

I just looked at him for a minute, thinking. What he said made a lot of sense. Tess was our friend. And I was so incredibly angry. I knew that I had a short temper and sometimes I flew off the handle for no reason, but this time I deserved to be mad, didn't I? I blocked out the little voice in my head that was saying, *Allie don't do it. You know it's wrong. There's another way.* I pretended not to hear. "Let's go," I said.

He pulled me by the arm and we took off down the street, determined to get our revenge, to set things straight. I didn't know where we were going or what our plan was, but I was mad, and I followed Holden, knowing that, right or wrong, we had just made a decision that would have an enormous impact. I don't think either of us really realized how big it would be.

As we ran, my mind was racing. That little voice in the back of my head was screaming, *What are you doing? Is this really what God would tell you to do? What would Miranda say?* My anger refused to listen. Jogging next to Holden, I could see his clenched jaw and the determined, almost zombie-like look in his eyes. I could tell that he had fought off his little voice too. There was no turning back now.

I realized that we were heading toward the school. I remembered seeing Chris and Trent skateboarding there many times. I was sure that was why Holden headed this way. We could see the schoolyard now, only a block away. There were a couple of figures on skateboards near the driveway entrance. Holden stopped suddenly and wiped the sweat off his forehead. It was turning out to be a really hot day. We should have been at the Golden Oaks pool or inside the air-conditioned library. Anywhere but where we were.

Holden looked at me and said seriously, "Allie, I'm going to confront those guys and whatever happens, happens."

"*You*? You mean *we*. You're not going alone," I answered, out of breath and a little annoyed. I wiped my face with my shirt and looked at him.

"Allie, come on now. I don't want you to get hurt. This isn't the place for a...." He stopped himself before he said "girl" and just looked at me pleadingly. He knew I considered it a dare when someone said something wasn't for girls, like basketball. But today I didn't even care. I just wanted to take care of this situation for Tess. We both did. I think that's why Holden didn't try to stop me when I insisted on going with him. He just shook his head in resignation.

In silence, we walked the last block to the schoolyard. I was nervous. Neither of us had ever done anything like this before. My stomach felt a little queasy, and when Holden ran his hands through his hair I could see that his hand was shaking. But we trudged on. Pictures of Tess crying in her kitchen kept flashing in my mind.

As we rounded the corner of the curved driveway, we could see Chris and Trent, now skateboarding over by the basketball courts. We picked up the pace and half jogged over to where they were. That little voice in my head—*What are you doing?*—kept trying to creep out, but I wouldn't let it. I couldn't listen to it now.

Chris, a stocky, mean-looking boy, saw us first. He stopped and stared at us, a surly grin on his round face. Trent was tall and broad-shouldered with the darkest hair and eyes I've ever seen. He realized what Chris was staring at and got off his skateboard. They came toward us. "Well, if it isn't the lovebirds," Trent sneered at us. "What can we do for you? Shouldn't you be off playing house or something?" Chris chuckled, now standing behind him.

"We're here for Tess, you jerks," I said. I could hardly contain my anger. "You need to leave her alone." My heart was beating fast, and it was getting harder and harder to breathe. I was scared, but I didn't care.

"What about Tess? Who's Tess?" asked Trent. And for a minute he looked innocent, and I thought, *Maybe we have the wrong kids. Maybe it wasn't them.*

But then Chris spoke up, "Yeah, you know Tess, Trent." And he nudged him with his elbow and started limping around with his left arm hanging at an odd angle at his side.

"Oh yeah, the retard with the arm. Yeah, we've gotten to know her real well this past year. Yeah, man, we write to each other. Consider us pen pals," Trent jeered. He began to laugh, and Chris joined in. Here we had it—almost a confession—and Holden and I were too dumbfounded, too shocked by their cruelty to say anything. We just stared at them, and I thought about how pathetic they were.

"What? Nothing to say, Cross?" Trent asked Holden, then turned to Chris. "Hey, I think we've offended the poor boy." Holden, now out of his shocked amazement stared coldly at Trent, who continued to taunt. "What? Your little girlfriend has to do all of the talking for you?"

Holden stood very still. His eyes, like blue ice, were squinted and focused solely on Trent. He took one slow and deliberate step toward Trent so he was no more than two inches away from his face and said, "Well, at least I'm not such a coward that I can't even sign my name to notes I send to defenseless girls."

This was too much for Trent. He pulled his right fist back and let it fly. It landed squarely on Holden's jaw with a horrible sound. Before I knew it, Chris had me pinned from behind. I struggled, landing one strong elbow in his ribs, but it was no contest. He had both my arms and I couldn't get free, but just to make sure, he stepped hard on my foot, grinding his heavy work boots into my toes. I flinched, trying to twist away, but he was too strong for me. All I could do was watch Trent and Holden trade punches. I was scared.

Trent and Holden circled one another, swinging and sometimes landing punches. Holden was strong and in shape, but I didn't think he could match Trent's punches for too much longer. Trent was good at this. He had done it dozens of times before. His lips were curled into what almost looked like a smile. *Could he be enjoying this?* I choked back a sob. There was a small cut above Holden's left eyebrow that was bleeding. I was crying now, and still struggling to get free. Tears blurred my view. I was glad that I couldn't clearly see the fighting. My stomach was churning at the sight and at the thought of what Holden and I had chosen to do. *What's going to happen now?*

Trent tackled Holden, and he went down with a thud. Just then, out of the corner of my eye, I saw a car turn into the schoolyard drive. *Thank God*, I thought. Chris had also seen the car. He pushed me down, skinning both my knees, and yelled to Trent, motioning to the car. Trent got up quickly, kicked Holden one last time in the ribs, and took off. They ran toward the schoolyard fence. I knew that the one thing they were afraid of was getting caught.

I scrambled up and ran to where Holden was now in a sitting

position on the asphalt, pressing his palm to the cut above his eyebrow. I knelt down and looked at Holden. He was really roughed up, with the makings of a black eye and a split lip. We both looked up as Trent screamed back to us, "You and your crippled friend better watch out at the festival. Just watch out!" Then they both were on the other side of the fence, running away from the approaching car. Holden and I looked at each other, bewildered.

The car pulled up to us. It was Miranda. She hurried out of the car, took one look at us, muttered a confused "What in the world?" and reached back into her glove box for some tissue. I reached down to help Holden stand up, and I saw that my hands were shaking. I was scared, now more than ever. Holden took my hand, got up, and looked at me. Wearily, he said, "What have we done, Allie?"

6

IT'S THAT SIMPLE

Miranda ran up to us. She looked confused and disappointed. "What were you doing?" she asked. "Fighting? Why? Are you guys okay?" Her eyes took inventory of all the scrapes and bruises on Holden and my skinned knees.

"We're fine," Holden managed to say.

"Get in," she said tightly.

Holden climbed into the front seat and I got in back, feeling like I was caught in a bad dream. As we rode, Holden explained to Miranda that we had gotten in a fight over something silly with Trent and Chris. I knew he wouldn't go into details about what really happened because of our promise to Tess. I felt so mixed up. I sat in the back seat with my forehead leaning on the window, too ashamed to meet Miranda's gaze in the rearview mirror. I just stared at the passing scenery, seeing nothing, thankful that Holden was doing the explaining.

As she drove, Miranda asked Holden a few questions. I could tell she knew there was more to the story than we were telling, but she didn't push too hard. Even after what she had seen us doing, it seemed like she trusted us. I'm not sure why. I felt so ashamed. As we rode, my mind was spinning with more questions than ever. More things eating away at me. *What did we do? How could we have made such a wrong choice? What are Chris and Trent planning to do at the festival? We've made everything worse. Now what do we do? Where are my answers from God?* I decided I needed to write in my prayer journal, so I composed an entry in my head.

> *Dear God,*
> *Help us. Holden and I didn't know what we*
> *were getting in to. Answer us, please.*

I was interrupted by Miranda. "Allie, I'm asking you a question," she said, as she turned toward the community center.

"I'm sorry, Miranda, what did you say?" I asked, sort of still in a daze. I was staring at the gashes on my knees, just now realizing that they hurt.

Miranda glanced back at me for a split second, then said, "Something is going on here that you're not telling me." She shook her head and then waited quietly for a response. Holden looked back at me and then looked away. We had tried to handle this ourselves and look where it had gotten us! I prayed about it and I still messed up. I wanted to tell Miranda everything, but instead I said nothing. I suddenly felt tears stinging my eyes. I wasn't proud of what Holden and I had done. Not at all.

We rode the rest of the way to the community center in silence. Miranda looked exasperated, yet she didn't press for any more details. I silently respected her for that. I sat looking out the window, trying to fight back guilty tears.

What should we do, God? Answer me, please.

At the community center, Miranda took us into the nurse's office and helped us clean up our injuries. Holden was washing off the cuts on his lip and above his eye. I poured peroxide over my scraped-up knees. Miranda came in and sat on the counter. She looked less annoyed now, but I knew she still wanted to talk to us. "Allie, Holden…I…um…I don't know why you were fighting or what is going on exactly, but I do know.…" She brushed a loose, flame-colored curl out of her eyes and gave us a serious look. "I do know that fighting is not the answer. What did it solve, you guys? Nothing. I can tell by the looks on your faces that it solved nothing. I thought you two would know better than that. All the times we've talked about this kind of stuff in Seekers.…" Her voice trailed off. She was shaking her head. She looked sort of hurt.

"Miranda," Holden began, "we do know better. It's just those stupid kids. We just got so mad." Holden looked ashamed.

I said, "We were just so angry. I know it's no excuse, but we had to do something. We couldn't just let them.…" I stopped myself before I gave away Tess's whole secret.

"I don't know what they did," said Miranda, "and you obviously don't want to tell me. That's fine. I'm not going to make you. But I personally think you should talk to someone. Maybe your parents." Miranda got up, signaling that she was ready to take us home and her questioning was coming to an end. However, she took one step closer to us, looked at us and asked, "Did you try praying?"

"Yes," Holden and I both cried at once.

"Of course," I continued. "I wrote all about it in my prayer journal. I kept asking God to answer me and tell me what to do. I needed some kind of guidance, a sign, something, Miranda. But I didn't get any." I was glad I had this chance to ask Miranda about this. I was so frustrated. I realized there were tears streaming down my face now.

"How do we know what we should do?" Holden asked quietly, finishing my thought for me.

"Follow Jesus' example." Miranda handed me a tissue from the nurse's desk and put her arm around me. "It's that simple."

"I know," said Holden, "but sometimes it's hard to know what that means." I understood what he meant. *Didn't Jesus want us to defend Tess?*

Miranda knelt in front of both of our chairs and looked up at us solemnly. "Y'know, I think you two did the right thing by praying about this, but I think you need to remember to seek out the answers God gives you. Sometimes you just need to look. God does answer."

Miranda got up, put out a hand for each of us, and pulled us to our feet. She said, "I want you to know that I'm always here if you need me. Think about what I said." She paused and looked at us each deeply in our eyes, almost like she was trying to read our thoughts. She turned quickly and said, "Come on. I'll take you home."

"We'll walk," I said. "Don't worry about taking us home."

Holden agreed.

"Don't forget about Seekers tonight, the meeting about the festival," Miranda reminded us. We assured her we wouldn't miss it, although I don't think either of us was very excited about this weekend's festivities anymore. We said our thanks and good-byes to Miranda and started on our way. I figured once we were alone we'd have a lot to talk about. But we walked in complete silence for almost 10 minutes. We had talked about it all already, I guess. I suppose we were both exhausted too. It was only about noon, but it felt much later.

When we got to May Street, I decided I needed to break the silence. "So, how are you going to explain your face?" I knew I wouldn't even need to explain the cuts on my knees. This kind of thing always happened when I was playing basketball. My mom wouldn't even ask. I was very glad I wasn't going to be in another position to lie.

"I think I'll just tell my mom it happened playing tackle football with the guys." Holden looked so defeated. "I just hate all this lying, Allie." We continued walking in silence.

When we turned onto Pinegrove, I knew I had to bring up the worst topic of all. The one thing we both had probably tried not to think about. "So what do you think they'll pull at the festival?" Visions of Tess crying flashed in my mind.

"I don't know. I just don't know." Holden looked weary, and I could tell that this wasn't what was on his mind. Something else was bothering him. A lot.

"What should we do?" I asked.

"Just listen for answers, like Miranda said."

I shook my head. "We sure didn't do that today," I said guilti-ly. "I'm sorry that I came over to your house all angry, Holden." I was feeling responsible for this whole thing.

"Allie," Holden said and stopped in his tracks. "We messed

up today. Bad decisions all around. Don't feel like it was all your fault."

Holden seemed so anxious. I could tell this wasn't the only thing he wanted to talk about. There was more troubling him. Then, he went on like he wasn't sure he should. He was looking at me with these intense blue eyes.

He grabbed my hand and his eyes searched mine. "Allie, all I kept thinking about while we were at the schoolyard was, 'What if they hurt Allie?' I mean not just scraped knees, but worse. That's the only thing that kept going through my mind. I don't know what I would've done."

I stood there dumbfounded, not knowing what to say. *What is Holden trying to say? Why is he holding my hand? Why do I like it?* When I didn't say anything, he let go of my hand and looked away, his cheeks turning a bright red. "Come on," he said. "Our moms are probably worried." He started walking quickly toward our houses.

I walked the rest of the way home with him in silence. I didn't know what to say. I was more confused than ever. As we got to Holden's driveway, he said, "See ya," without even looking at me, turned, and ran up his stairs.

"Holden, I…." I yelled at him. I didn't know what to say, but I didn't want to leave like this.

"Forget it, Al. It's okay," he called and he was inside.

I didn't know what to think or feel about the fight, about Tess, or even about the past five minutes with Holden. So much to think about. I was feeling so mixed up. *What is happening? What just happened with Holden and me?* Although so much had happened today, nothing was figured out. Things just seemed worse.

7

A Long, Lonesome Walk

I slowly plodded up my front steps and turned my key in the door. When I walked into the kitchen, I found a note from my mom saying she had gone to run some errands and would be back sometime that afternoon. I was glad to be alone. I needed to think, to sort things out.

I got some cookies out of the pantry and poured myself a tall glass of milk. I took the food with me up to my bedroom, set it on my milk-crate night table, and plopped on my bed. As I unlaced my gym shoes and threw them into my closet, I thought about all the strange things that had happened today. I knew Holden and I shouldn't have gone looking for that fight. I mean, I knew it all along, but now we were in for it at the festival. There had to be a better way to stick up for Tess. I just had to figure out how to listen for God's answers. I took out my prayer journal and began to write.

Dear God, help me to hear your answers. Help me to listen.

I wrote an entire page in my journal. I explained all of my thoughts, everything that happened today, and what all of my questions were. I wrote about Tess, the fight, Holden, and everything else. When I finally put my pen down, I felt a lot better. It was as if I had just gotten rid of some of the heavy weight on my shoulders.

I put my journal away and polished off the last of the cookies and milk. I curled up on my bed, realizing just how exhausted I really was. And my thoughts drifted to Holden. I thought about what he had said—how he was worried about me. *Was he trying to tell me he liked me?* I realized the whole time he was fighting, I was scared, too, that he'd get hurt. *But that's just because he's my friend, right? Then how come I liked it when he held my hand?* It felt…well, exciting. And lately when I thought about Holden, my stomach felt like it was on a roller coaster. *What does that mean?* I was so sleepy now. I was having trouble keeping my eyes open. My mind drifted into a state of half-sleeping, half-waking. Trent's nasty laughter and mocking smile plagued my dreams.

BAM! BAM! BAM! I jumped out of bed. *I must have dozed off*, I thought. I figured I had dreamed that someone was knocking at the front door. But there it was again—BAM! BAM! BAM! Whoever was there was being very impatient. I ran down the stairs, still not fully awake.

I opened the door. It was Rebecca. I started to say hello, but she didn't even give me a chance. She stormed into the living room, dropped her backpack on the floor, and started pacing. "Allison Johansen, I can't believe you!" she shrieked. I shut the door and sat on the couch. She continued, "What were you two thinking? Ben told me all about it. Fighting with Chris and Trent? What did you think that was going to do?" She raised her eyebrows and looked at me. She didn't wait for an answer. "I'll tell you what it did: nothing! Nothing but get us into more trouble! Now they're going to do something at the festival! What were you thinking, Allie?"

I wanted to explain to her that she was right, to say that I was sorry, but she wasn't finished yet. "I know your heart was in the right place, Al. You wanted to defend Tess. Fine. We all were mad. But fighting? Why?" She stopped pacing, put her hands on her hips, and stared at me.

I shrugged helplessly. Here was my chance to explain, but I didn't know how. "I didn't know what else to do, Rebecca. I needed some help, some answers." I knew how pathetic it sounded, but it was true.

"Help? Answers?" Rebecca echoed. "What about me? I tried to reason with you! Sometimes, Allie, you choose the answers you listen to." She seemed so disappointed in me, and I felt so ashamed. I knew what we had done was wrong, but that wasn't all I needed to know. I still didn't know how to listen for the right answers. I wanted to know how to deal with those jerks another way, a way that would work. I was so confused, so ashamed. I wanted to explain it all to Rebecca, but I didn't know where to start. *How should I begin?* I tried to think of the right words, but nothing came. So I sat there and didn't say anything.

Rebecca grabbed her backpack and stormed out.

I sat on the couch and stared after her, stunned. *What should I do? What should I do about Trent and Chris and the festival?*

About Holden? About Rebecca? I needed answers. I needed to listen.

I sat there in the living room for a long time and just thought. Yesterday morning all that mattered to me was going to the dance tomorrow night and the festival on Saturday. Now I had so much more to worry about. So many things had changed. Holden and I had really messed things up. Rebecca was mad at me, and I was sure Tess was too. Trent and Chris were still plotting against Tess and probably the rest of us too. Then, to top it off, the one person I really needed to talk to about all of this was Holden, and even he was acting strange. There was too much to think about. Miranda had told me to listen. That's what I didn't do before. But what was I supposed to listen to?

My mom came home before too long with a mushroom-and-tomato pizza for dinner. My favorite. We sat in the kitchen and ate. I guess I was unusually quiet because halfway through the first piece, my mom asked, "So, what's bothering you, Alliecakes?" I thought about how Holden always called me that.

"Nothing, Mom," I began. "It's just…." I really wanted to tell her everything, but I knew I had made a promise to Tess. Still, Miranda had said we should tell someone and I was beginning to think so too. This was getting too serious for us to keep from all of the adults involved. I thought for a second and made a promise to myself. *If we don't get this fixed by tomorrow night, I will tell Mom, regardless of what I promised Tess.* I knew we couldn't just wait for something awful to happen at the festival.

I continued, "Mom, it's just that I had a fight with Rebecca and with Holden too." It wasn't the complete truth, but it wasn't a lie either. It was the best I could do. She gave me some motherly advice and let it drop. I wasn't sure whether she believed my story, but at this point I took what I could get. I was just thankful she didn't push for too many details.

After dinner I watched some TV and felt pretty lonely. Mom came in and reminded me that I had a Seekers meeting at 6:30. I had completely forgotten about it. This was probably the first time in my life that I wasn't really excited about going. I considered not going at all, but I knew that we would be planning for the dance and the festival. I knew I should be there for that.

I went up to my room, combed my hair, and put on a clean pair of jean shorts and a T-shirt. As I was slipping on my sandals, I looked up at the clock. It was a little after 6:00 and no one had called or shown up. We always walked together to the community center. We would call each other about this time to say where we'd meet up, even though it was inevitably at the corner of Pinegrove and Grand Boulevard. As I headed downstairs, I was feeling lonelier than ever. I decided to wait a few minutes to see whether Holden would come over to get me or whether Rebecca would call.

At 6:15, I was still sitting at the kitchen table. My mom was doing the dishes. I decided to head to the community center on my own, and I stood up to go. "Mom, I'm going to Seekers."

She turned and gave me a concerned look. I knew that she was aware that the usual routine with my friends had been broken. "Are you going all by yourself, Allie?" she asked hesitantly.

"Yeah, I'll be fine though," I answered. She walked over and gave me a hug. I hugged her back, probably a little too hard, but I really needed it.

"You know, you can always talk to me, Al," she said. I

looked at her and nodded.

"I know, Mom. I'll see you after Seekers." I turned and went out the back door. I was so glad I had resolved to tell my mom tomorrow night. If we couldn't get this figured out on our own, I had to let her know. We would need help making sure no one got hurt in any way at the festival.

The evening air was thick and humid. It weighed on me as I walked through my yard and onto the sidewalk. Crickets chirped, and the first lightning bugs of the night flitted from yard to yard. I looked up at Holden's house as I passed it, hoping to see him bound down the steps toward me, but he wasn't there. I peered into the dusky evening toward the corner of Pinegrove and Grand, hoping that everyone would be standing there waiting for me, but they weren't. In the back of my mind, I knew that most of my friends were probably going to Seekers alone tonight, but at that moment it didn't comfort me very much. I felt utterly alone.

When I arrived at the community center, I quickly scoped out the crowd. I saw Tess and Rebecca first. They were sitting together and talking. They both looked up, saw me, and resumed their conversation. My heart sank when this happened. *I knew they were going to be mad at me, but the silent treatment?* I sat down in a folding chair far across the circle from them and just waited for the meeting to begin.

Holden and Ben came in a minute later. Ben saw me right away, waved, and smiled. Holden looked up and saw me too. The cut above his eye looked better already. I held my breath, waiting to see whether he would acknowledge me. *Will he still speak to me after everything that happened today?* He waved slightly, turned around, and found a couple of seats for him and Ben—nowhere near me. *Okay, not as bad as I thought.*

Some kids from my computer class last year sat in the seats next to me. I talked to them a little and basically just waited for the Seekers meeting to end. I wished I hadn't come, but I knew that I owed it to Miranda, the festival, and my friends—or at least my ex-friends. *How did things get so messed up in the matter of one day?* Yesterday we had all been goofing around in the town square and now, here we were.

I tried to pay attention to the meeting, but my thoughts were on everything else. I tuned in long enough to volunteer for cleanup at the dance, and then I let my thoughts wander.

I was deep in thought, picturing myself at the carnival doing the milk-bottle toss all by myself, when the kid next to me nudged me with his elbow. It was time for the closing prayer. I bowed my head and folded my hands.

Miranda began, "Lord, put your blessing on all the festivities this weekend. Keep us all safe. Also, help us to follow your lead daily, Lord. Help us to know how to do that. Amen."

There's no way to know for sure who Miranda had in mind when she said that closing prayer, but it sure sounded like she had said it on behalf of Holden and me. I was glad. We needed all the help we could get.

When a friend from computer class offered me a ride home with his mom, I accepted right away. I definitely didn't feel like another long, lonesome walk.

8

MY GReat
IDea

I woke up the next morning and the first thing I thought was, "Cool! Today's the dance!" And for a second, I was all excited. Just for a second. Then I remembered everything that had happened the day before. But I felt rejuvenated by the night's sleep, and I was thinking more clearly. A lot of things needed to be fixed, like my friendships with Holden, Rebecca, and Tess, for example. However, I had one thing that was much more important: finding a way to defend Tess and my friends from Chris and Trent. The festival was tomorrow night, and there was no telling what they would pull.

I changed into a T-shirt and shorts, put on my gym shoes, and went for my morning jog. When I went through the school-yard, I cringed a little. As I was jogging, I thought about the dance. A big part of me really wanted to go and enjoy myself. I had been waiting for this day for a long time. It was the biggest event for kids my age in the summer. All my friends would be there. But as I jogged around the track and started to head for home, I realized that going to the dance couldn't be my priority today.

First of all, I had a lot of thinking to do. I had to figure out how to handle Chris and Trent's threats about the festival. I knew that they would be at the festival and they would be up to their dirty tricks, but I didn't think they would go to the dance. They thought they were too cool to be seen there. So I didn't have to worry about that. But I did need to prepare for tomorrow. I would just have to forget about going to the dance. And, if last night's Seekers meeting was any kind of indication, my friends probably would barely acknowledge my existence at the dance. What fun would that be? I had to come up with a new plan that maybe—just maybe—would help set things right with my friends and we could get back to normal.

As I jogged up my front porch steps, I was happy with my new resolution. Even though I knew it would be more fun to go to the dance with my friends, I hoped that things were going to start looking up. They had to. Jogging always gave me time to think and helped me see the bright side. I went inside and took the stairs two at a time.

I took my time showering, brushing my teeth, and getting dressed. I made my way down the stairs.

My mom was in the kitchen drinking a cup of coffee. She looked up. "Hey, Allie." She looked me up and down. I knew she was about to critique my clothes.

"What's wrong with what I'm wearing, Mom?" I feigned annoyance, but I actually didn't care when she commented on the way I dressed. It was kind of like a game. She was pretty cool about my clothes.

"Well, isn't the dance tonight, Al? Cut-off jeans and a tank top might not cut it."

"Mom, it's a teen dance. We just wear whatever we want."

Mom smiled mischievously. "Well, don't you want to wear that one light blue dress I bought you last year?" She was kidding—at least I hoped she was.

"Mom, you can't be serious. That thing has more ruffles than a wedding dress!" We both laughed. "Besides, Mom, I don't think I'm going to go anyway." I looked away, knowing that this comment would make her suspicious. She would definitely want to know what was up now.

"Why, Allie? Because of the problems you had with Rebecca and Holden?"

I didn't say anything. I was rummaging around in the fridge for an apple, taking longer than necessary just to avoid her questions and her gaze.

After a few seconds, she gathered that she was right and went on. "I'm sure they're over it already, Al. In fact, Holden was over here looking for you when you went jogging this morning."

"He was?" I asked. I turned around and looked at Mom, suddenly uninterested in the fridge. "What did he say?" I couldn't believe that he wasn't still mad at me for yesterday. He had practically poured his heart out to me, and I had just stood there like a dork. I mean, I think that's what had happened anyway.

Mom looked at me, a little surprised at my excitement. "Well, he just said that he would talk to you later at the dance, because he was going over to Ben's for the day." I must have looked awfully disappointed because Mom added, "He did seem bummed that you weren't here, you know. So maybe you should go to the dance after all." She gave me a quizzical look.

I nodded. I knew she wanted me to explain everything, but I couldn't. Not yet. I knew that I did have to go to the dance now. Maybe Holden had thought of what we should do about Chris and Trent, or maybe he just wanted to talk to me. Either way, I had to see him. I was a little surprised at how much I wanted to see him.

For the rest of the day, I helped my mom around the house, partly to be a good daughter and partly to help the time pass as quickly as possible. I couldn't wait for the dance. At 5:00, I went upstairs and got ready. I put on my favorite semi-dressy outfit— white jean shorts and a blue cotton shirt with little white flowers on it. I brushed my hair and decided to leave it down for once. I even opened a tube of raspberry lip gloss—a birthday gift from Rebecca—and dabbed a little on my lips. I took one last look in the mirror, grabbed my sandals, and trotted down the stairs.

Mom did a double take when she saw me. "Looking good, Alliecakes," she said.

Mom offered to drive me over to the center. She was going to the grocery store and it was on the way. I accepted, glad to avoid walking alone to the community center. On the way there, I kept telling myself that I was just excited to talk to Holden about what we were going to do about the festival, but deep down I knew it was more than that.

I walked into the community center and couldn't believe how the place had been transformed. The decorating committee certainly had done its job. The theme was "Under the Sea."

There were all different kinds of paper sea animals hanging from the ceiling—starfish, squid, dolphins. Blue construction-paper waves ran along the walls covered with tiny white Christmas lights glowing from inside fish nets. The place looked great.

As I walked in, the DJ was playing some reggae music, and I was really glad that I had come. I didn't see any of my friends yet, so I walked toward the food table. I grabbed some punch and decided to walk around and see all of the scenery. I ran into the kids from my computer class and I talked to them for a while. While I chatted, my gaze wandered to the dance floor.

Ben was in the middle of a crowd, lip-syncing dramatically to a ballad by the latest boy band. I smiled in spite of myself. I spotted Rebecca dancing with a tall boy, laughing and talking, looking like she was really enjoying it. When they turned around, I peered through the crowd, trying to get a closer look at her newest flame. One of his eyes was slightly black and blue. My heart sank as I realized who it was. It was Holden. My Holden.

My Holden? What am I thinking? I excused myself from my conversation with the computer kids and took a seat at an empty table in the corner. *Why does seeing Holden and Rebecca dancing together bother me so much?*

Suddenly I realized someone was walking toward me. It was Tess, sweet, understanding Tess. I knew she was probably still mad at me for the whole deal yesterday in the schoolyard, but here she was. She could probably see I really needed a friend. I don't think I was ever happier to see her. I wanted to tell her everything, explain myself. I needed to talk to someone about everything that happened yesterday.

"You know," she said quietly as she sat down beside me, "the only reason Rebecca is dancing with him is to make you jealous. She wants you to realize that you like him, and yeah, she's probably still a little peeved at you 'cause of yesterday."

I was so happy to have someone to talk to, I just started to ramble. "I don't care about that. I mean, I do, but that's not important right now. I know that you heard all about the fight yesterday, and I'm sorry. I truly am. I've been thinking about it a lot. I just was so angry and I needed so badly to help you. Holden and I made a bad decision. We didn't know what we were getting ourselves into, with Chris and Trent's new threat and all. I mean, we just made it worse." I stopped a second to catch my breath.

Tess was listening intently. She motioned for me to keep going.

"I've been thinking about it a lot. I know it was wrong to get in that fight. I wanted God to guide me in the right direction. I was actually expecting to get an answer somehow, some way. And then when I didn't, I guess I just let my anger get the best of me. I don't know. I've been trying to figure out what we should do about Trent and Chris tomorrow and I've been thinking and praying and I don't know. I don't want to tell my mom, but, Tess, I just don't know what else to do. I guess I've learned that God doesn't answer us the way I want...."

"Hey, wait a minute. You shouldn't think that. There are so many ways that God answers us. You just have to know where to look." Tess looked at me intently.

I asked, "What do you mean? Everybody says that."

"Aren't there times when you just know what the right decision is?" Tess asked.

"Well, yeah, sometimes."

"Well, then you know what it is like to feel sure about something," Tess replied. "That's God helping you know through your conscience. I know that not every decision is that easy. But, don't you sometimes feel like you can hear someone in the back of your head telling you what to do?"

"Yes," I answered. I remembered the little voice that I had ignored on our way to the schoolyard yesterday.

Tess continued, "That's God, Allie. God helps you think through your actions and make the right decisions. That's how God answers you."

I was beginning to understand. It was sort of like the answer was right there, in the back of my mind, waiting for me to acknowledge it. "Tess, I know exactly what you mean. Even yesterday when I decided to go to the schoolyard, I knew it wasn't the right decision, just the only one that I could think of right then." Now it all seemed so clear to me.

I continued, "And God was trying to help me through you guys. I mean, that was God when Rebecca kept telling me not to go. If I had stopped and thought about Seekers or Miranda, I probably would've realized how wrong it was. Miranda told me yesterday after it all happened that we should follow Jesus' example. Maybe we need to reread all those Bible stories again. Then maybe we could learn how to deal with this stuff the way Jesus would." I felt like a 10-pound dumbbell had just been lifted off each of my shoulders.

Tess looked at me and smiled. "See, God does answer you. It might not be obvious, but God does answer."

I jumped out of my seat, thanked her, and gave her a hug.

Just then Rebecca, Holden, and Ben walked up. I couldn't resist. I got up and greeted each of them with a monstrous hug and a smile. "You guys," I said excitedly, "I want to say I'm sorry for everything yesterday." I looked at Holden and said, "I mean everything." I just wanted to start fresh with everyone. "We need to band together right now more than ever."

"I'm sorry too, guys, for getting in that fight," Holden said, pointing at the fading blue mark under his eye. "No matter how much they deserved it, fighting only made things worse. I'm not going to let my anger get the best of me anymore."

I looked at Holden and silently promised myself that I would discuss everything I had just figured out with him next time I had the chance.

"I suppose we can let it slide this time, Cross," Ben said. "But I think you deserve about a thousand hours of community service."

"What do you mean?" Tess questioned.

"You know, community service to repay society for the wrongs he's done." The curl of a smile began to form on Ben's face. "Holden, you can start your hours by mowing my lawn on Thursdays, hauling out my garbage cans on Monday mornings, massaging my cheesy feet after soccer practice, and…."

"Gross!" I cried, shaking my head and pinching my nose in feigned disgust. We laughed and exchanged grossed-out looks.

"Nice try, Benny, but don't hold your breath," Holden teased.

"You may want to hold your breath with those feet," Rebecca added.

"Seriously, all is forgiven, guys, even without the punishment," Tess said. "Right, everybody?"

Holden smiled at me, and Rebecca put her arm around me and squeezed. Everyone nodded and agreed to go back to normal, happy to have the arguments behind us.

Rebecca pinched my cheek and told me I looked nice. She gave me a hug and whispered, "Sorry, I tried to make you jealous."

I had already forgiven her. But we didn't have time to think about that right now. We had to get started. Even though I wasn't positive what we were about to do, I knew that it was important we do it. We had a mission.

"Guys, we have got to get started," I announced in my most teacherly voice.

"Yes, Professor Johansen." Ben bowed slightly, but winked at me as he straightened.

I motioned for everyone to sit around the round table in the corner of "the sea." This was the perfect meeting place. I had to explain what was going through my mind, so I continued.

"See, yesterday Holden and I made a bad decision. We wanted to defend Tess and teach those jerks a lesson, but we went about it wrong."

I took a rubber band out of my pocket and pulled my hair into a ponytail. I meant business.

"I've been praying about this and trying to figure out what we should have done. Now, you know that Chris and Trent are planning on doing something at the festival tomorrow. So we need to decide what we should do. Tess and I were talking and I think I finally figured it out. I know how to find the answers."

Ben asked, "Well, what is it, Allie? What should we do?"

"Well, it's not that easy. I don't know the answer, but I do know how God wants us to find it."

Holden chimed in. "And it's not by going up to talk to Trent and Chris at the schoolyard," We all laughed.

"Right," I said. "We need to put our minds together, and we need to think about Jesus' example. We need to listen to each other's advice." I looked at Rebecca when I said this, and she smiled.

Tess, normally so soft-spoken, slapped her hand on the table and said boldly, "I think I have an idea." She looked almost as surprised as we did. "Well, you know how they have the stage set up in the town square for the auction and the dancing tomorrow night?" We nodded. "Maybe we could get Miranda to, like, make some sort of a speech about treating others with respect or something."

It was a good idea. We all nodded and encouraged Tess. It sounded like it could work. We had to reach Chris and Trent somehow, and maybe Miranda would do it for us.

Then, I had a great idea.

"I have an even better way that we could get our message across!" I shouted, almost jumping out of my seat.

"How, Allie?" Rebecca asked excitedly.

"Why don't *we* do the speech? Better yet, why don't we put on a variety show with skits and stuff to get our point across?"

"Allie, you're a genius!" said Ben. He loved being on stage. I knew he'd like the idea.

Holden spoke up. "Yeah, that sounds awesome. We could get everyone in Seekers to help out. It sounds like fun too."

"Is this going to be my big break?" Rebecca asked, batting

her eyes and patting her hair. "Allie, really…that's a great idea."

Tess seemed less excited than the rest of us. In fact, she looked a little scared. But after all she had been through with Chris and Trent, who could blame her? She asked timidly, "I don't have to get up on stage, do I?"

We immediately shook our heads and told her she didn't have to if she didn't want to. After she heard this, she perked right up. She added, "Hey, maybe I could help with the scripts for some of the skits, though." She pulled out a little notebook from her pocket and started jotting down notes.

Rebecca grabbed my arm. "Allie, you guys.…" We looked at her. "We only have until tomorrow afternoon to get this ready."

We were quiet for a minute, taken aback. Then Rebecca piped up again. "So, we'd better get started."

We all laughed. We were going to do this.

I looked around the table at my friends and thought to myself, *Now* this *is God's answer to me. This is what God wants us to do.* And I knew it was. I could feel it.

We spent the rest of the dance recruiting other Seekers members. We explained about the show and what kind of skits we had in mind, but we didn't tell anybody about Tess or Trent and Chris, because we didn't think we needed to. We were all so excited when we explained our idea, the other kids couldn't resist.

Our idea started out small, but by the end of the night we had kids who were going to paint scenery, other kids who had amplifiers and microphones, and still other kids who had costumes we could use. Almost everyone wanted to be part of one of the skits, which was great. We needed all the help that we could get.

When the dance ended, my friends and I met to discuss what we needed to get ready for tomorrow. We planned for everyone to be at the square at 9:00 A.M. sharp, with the show being at 3:00 P.M.

"Oh no!" Tess cried. "We have forgotten one important thing. We have to ask Miranda's permission to use the stage tomorrow afternoon, and she'll have to chaperone us tomorrow morning. We've got to talk to her."

We sat there dumbfounded for a second. How could we have made all these plans without asking first? I guess we were just too excited. We knew we had to ask, but we fidgeted because no one wanted to be the one to ask Miranda, simply because she would want details we weren't free to give.

Tess saw this in our faces. "We can tell her everything guys. I don't care. I trust her."

"I'll go do it," I said, not hesitating a second now. I glanced around the emptying community center, searching for Miranda's red hair. I spotted her cleaning up the food table. Crossing the room, I started gathering up paper cups and napkins.

She looked up and saw that it was me. "Hi, Allie. I saw that you and your friends were awfully busy with something tonight, and you have that 'I need something' look on your face. What's up?" she asked cheerfully.

I quickly explained everything that went on with Trent and Chris and Tess, our fight, and our new plan. Miranda was, of course, appalled at Chris and Trent, and she commended me for my new plan of attack and agreed to help us out. "I even have some books of skits you might want to take a look at. You guys might get some ideas."

I was so happy, I gave her a quick hug and thanked her from the bottom of my heart.

She said, "Come on. I'll get the books from my office right now."

I followed her. I still had something to talk to her about.

"Miranda," I said, a little shy about going on, but needing to, "I just want you to know that I really learned a lot through this whole mess, and, well, thanks."

"Your actions show how much you've learned. And I'm glad you've learned it." Miranda smiled, handed me the books, and said, "You listened. It works."

I found everybody finishing the cleanup. We quickly collected all the garbage and put everything away so we could get going and talk about our big plans. We were so wound up about tomorrow that we were interrupting each other as ideas tumbled out. We decided on jobs that each of us had to get done.

Tess was already working on a script for our skit. She began to thumb through the books Miranda had given us. Rebecca and I were going to make a banner. The boys were going to make flyers to post everywhere early in the morning—windshields, lamp posts, bulletin boards.

We were on our way to making a difference. The excitement in the air was almost tangible. We had even come up with a name: The Seekers Extravaganza. We giggled at how corny it sounded, but I knew that it somehow fit.

As we walked home in the night air, I noticed that some of the stars were just coming out. I took a deep breath and looked around at my friends. *It doesn't get any better than this*, I thought.

Rebecca and I decided to meet at my house at 7:00 A.M. to

get started on the banner, so that we could be at the square ready to rehearse by 9:00. I realized that there was no way I would be able to fall asleep tonight. I was way too excited!

9

THIS WAS OUR DAY

At about 6:00 A.M. I awoke to the sound of birds chirping outside my window. It had been a restless night's sleep, and I was glad to see daylight. I sat up and grabbed my prayer journal. I flipped through it and skimmed over my entries. I had definitely learned a lot in the past few days. I decided I needed to write another prayer—a happier one.

> *Dear God,*
> *I just wanted to say thank you for helping me*
> *understand where to find you and for giving me the*
> *strength to forgive Chris and Trent. I realize now it's*
> *more important for us to teach them your ways*
> *than to pick a fight with them. Thanks for all*
> *that I've learned lately. And, hey, we could really*
> *use some help whipping this show together today.*
> *Bless us! Amen*

With that, I put my journal back on my nightstand and jumped out of bed, ready to face the world. I was so excited about our show today, I could barely stand it. As I bounded down the stairs, I decided to skip my morning jog. I had too many other things to worry about. When I got to the kitchen, my mom was already up drinking coffee. She was sketching something on a notepad at the kitchen table.

"Good morning, early bird," she said as she looked up at me. Last night, I had told my mom all about the show in the square today and why the message of our show was to be about accepting people with differences. I had left out the details. I hadn't named Tess, but I did confess my fighting. I'm sure Mom gathered enough from the conversation to fill in any holes. She didn't push for too much information, and that made it easier to tell her about stuff. We had stayed up and talked for more than an hour about what had happened, about my choices, and about plans for the big show. Mom had been full of ideas, and I went to bed knowing she'd be up early to help Rebecca and me this morning.

"So, Mom, what do you think we should do?" I asked as I grabbed an orange and sat next to her.

"Well, Allie, this morning I sewed two old white sheets together that could make an excellent banner. I thought you'd need at least two to get the whole title on there in big enough letters: 'The Seekers Extravaganza.' You know, it does have a nice ring to it." She smiled and scooted the notepad toward me where she had sketched a couple of different ways to make our banner. They looked fantastic.

"Thanks, Mom! I'm so excited," I said, peeling my orange

and stuffing the first juicy pieces into my mouth. "This is going to be great. I just hope a lot of people come. Do you think they will?"

Mom looked at me with some concern. "Well, Allie, you know it is sort of short notice, with you guys putting up the flyers and things only this morning."

"You're right," I said, and heard the disappointment in my own voice.

"But, you know what I could do," she said with a sly smile. "I could get on the phone and call some other teachers and PTA parents and get them to make some phone calls. I think we could get the word out that way."

"That sounds awesome, Mom!" I hugged her. Everything was working out so well.

Mom looked at her watch and said, "Allie, you'd better get upstairs and get ready. Rebecca will be here soon. I'll go get the sheets and the paints and set the stuff up on the driveway for you two. After I shower, I'll get to work on the phone."

Before 7:00 I heard someone knocking at the front door. With my hair still wrapped in a towel, I ran downstairs. "Hey, Rebecca," I said.

Before I could get another word out, she walked into the kitchen, saying, "Well, I thought we could use some tempera paints. I put them in my backpack. I also brought some glitter. That will definitely be eye-catching, and that's what we want. We could go with primary colors, but, hey, why not mix it up a little—neons could work." She went on and on.

I loved it. This painting stuff was right up her alley and I enjoyed her enthusiasm. "My mom had a few ideas. She put them on that notepad on the table," I said, using the towel to finish drying my hair. We sat down at the kitchen table and Rebecca eyed my mom's plans. I grabbed a rubber band off the counter and put up my hair.

"Looks good, Allie." She pointed at one of my mom's ideas. "I think we should definitely do this 3-D job." It looked like all of the letters in The Seekers Extravaganza were jumping out at you. I nodded in agreement. It would look really cool. Rebecca continued, "Now, I think we should outline the letters in glitter and...."

As we walked outside, we discussed colors. There was a lot to be done, and we were brimming with energy and enthusiasm. The sheets were lying on the driveway with stones holding them down in each corner. My mom had set out a few paints and brushes that were left over from the touch-up painting we did on the house last summer. Rebecca dumped out her backpack. She had more colors than the rainbow.

We worked for more than an hour without a word. My mom came out to see how we were doing, and we actually stopped for a second and took a step back to look at our banner. It was turning out well. No, better than that—it looked terrific! Mom even said that it looked professional. Rebecca and I traded high fives and got back to work.

Around 8:30 Rebecca and I were cleaning out our brushes and picking up paints when we saw Holden and Ben walking toward us with a stack of flyers in their hands. It looked as if they had been as busy as we were.

Holden raced up to our banner to get a good look. "You

guys, this is phenomenal!" he said, his mouth open in a look of surprise.

Ben was right behind him. "Man, you guys are awesome."

Rebecca and I just beamed, loving the acceptance of our first major artwork together.

Holden handed me one of their flyers. "Would you like to come to our variety show at the square this afternoon, miss?" he asked comically.

I took a look at the flyer. "Hey, did you guys make these flyers? They look pretty professional too," I said, handing it to Rebecca so she could see it.

"Don't sound so surprised," said Ben laughing. "We designed it on my computer."

"These are good," said Rebecca. "Did you get them up all over the place?"

"Hey," Holden said, "by now everyone in Golden Oaks is staring at one of these."

Ben nodded. "Yeah, and we put one in every store window, on every parked car, and on every telephone pole. I even tied one around the neck of my neighbor's golden retriever. And my brother's wearing one on his back that he doesn't even know about."

"You know," I said with a smile, "if all the kids who said they would help are even doing half as much as we are, this thing is going to rock!"

Rebecca nodded. "Yeah, and I can't wait to get on stage and do our skit."

Ben, Golden Oaks's budding actor, chimed in, "Yeah, where's Tess? I want to read the script." He was eager to get on that stage too. We all were, for Tess's sake.

As if on cue, Tess came around the corner of the house, a pile of papers in her hands and a couple of overstuffed bags over her shoulder. "Just came from The Copy Kingdom, guys. I copied a script for everyone. Typed it up last night, and I brought all the props we need," she said quietly and motioned to her stuffed bags. She started handing out the papers. She saw our banner and stopped dead in her tracks. "Wow, you guys! This is so cool! I love the 3-D effect. The rainbow colors are so bright and the glitter is super!"

When Tess finished handing out the copies of the script, we leafed through it. Tess, our director because she refused to be in the skit, told us to read through it quickly before we left for the square to rehearse.

I sat down on the driveway and read. The script gave me goose bumps. When everyone was finished, I said, only half joking, "This is award-winning material." We congratulated Tess on her writing efforts and decided we'd better get going to the town square. We had a lot of rehearsing to do, not to mention coordinating all the other kids and their acts.

We each picked up a side of the banner. We had to walk with it out in front of us like we were in a parade because it wasn't dry yet. It was sort of clumsy. We agreed that it was good advertising, though!

Ben caught his shoe on one of the corners of the banner and fell down, right into a somersault.

"That must get a 10, ladies and gentleman," he announced as he blew kisses to an imaginary audience. We laughed giddily. We were so excited about our big day.

About halfway to the town square, Tess stopped abruptly and said, "Guys, I…um…I have to tell you.…" She looked upset.

Oh no, I thought. Not another note. *Please, no more harassing.* But I knew it had happened again, simply by the look on her face. We had been so excited about the performance today, we had forgotten why we decided to do it in the first place.

Tess continued. "I got another e-mail today about not coming to the festival. And they mentioned our show too." She looked like she was going to cry. She pulled a piece of paper out of her back pocket and handed it to Ben. "I printed out the e-mail. I figured you guys had a right to know. Besides, we're all done with secrets," she said firmly.

Ben read the e-mail out loud. "Tess, We hope we don't see your crippled self at the festival. And tell your friends not to count on pulling off this stupid show either." Ben crumpled up the e-mail and shoved it into his pocket.

We all stood there, deflated.

I looked at each of my friends and said, "We can't let them do this. We were so excited about our idea. We're not scared of them. We've got to show them what is right. And this time we're doing it the right way."

"Yeah," Holden agreed. "Let's forget about them. We have a great message to put out there today, a message that everyone needs to hear, especially Trent and Chris. Let them *try* to stop us. We have to do this, guys. So, hey—the show must go on!"

We started walking toward the town square again. We held the banner high so everyone could see it. This was our day.

10

THE SHOW MUST GO ON

When we got to the town square, it was already buzzing with activity and excitement. The custodians from the community center were setting up folding chairs in front of the stage. They seemed to be expecting a lot of people. There were groups of kids dispersed about the square, rehearsing their skits. Scenery was being put together on the stage. Some high school kids were testing lights and hooking up microphones. Our technical crew was figuring out how to open and close the big red curtain on the stage that stood about five feet high. Some younger kids were modeling costumes for their friends. It looked like a Broadway production in the works.

Ben and Holden decided to put the banner at the very top of the stage, above the curtain and the lights. Rebecca, Tess, and I left them to their work and went to find Miranda. We found her behind the stage working with the Explorers group, the third through fifth graders. They were evidently going to sing for the show.

When she saw us coming toward her, Miranda gave the kids a five-minute break and walked toward us. She looked eager to speak with us. "How's it going? Are you ready to rehearse?" she asked.

"We're ready to go," I exclaimed.

"Well," Miranda said, "I had all of the groups of kids report to me as they got here. I think everybody has shown up now. I've put together a rehearsal schedule so that you know when you have the stage to rehearse. It's posted backstage. I think I'm going to stick to the same order for the actual show. I put you guys right at the end. End the show on a high note, I thought." She gave us a big smile.

We were so happy to have Miranda helping us. She knew how to do all the grunt work and organization. It just made everything so much easier for us. We thanked her and were about to leave when Janie, a sixth grader, came running up to Miranda.

"Miranda, Miranda, come quick," she said, tugging at Miranda's sleeve and gasping for breath. We all followed Janie backstage and immediately saw what had caused the ruckus. On one of the pieces of scenery that was painted with trees and park benches, someone had painted the words "WATCH OUT DORKS!" with green paint. Several kids had gathered around to see what was going on. The words were sloppy, but there was an obvious similarity in handwriting to the note Tess had received on her bike. It's not like we wouldn't have known who it was anyway.

Miranda quickly sprang into action while we stood there, our mouths gaping. "Just a silly prank, kids," Miranda said light-heartedly, yet I could detect the worry in her voice. She quickly took a rag out of her pocket and attempted to wipe off the ridiculous threat. The rag simply smeared the still-wet words. The scenery was ruined, but at least none of the other kids would have to read the message.

After most of the other kids had left the scene of the crime, I said quietly, "Miranda, do you think we should go through with this?" I desperately wanted her to say yes, but I felt I had to ask.

"Of course we're going through with it." Miranda looked astonished at the question, and I was glad that she didn't want to give in to those bullies.

Rebecca piped up, "We can't let these troublemakers decide what we can and cannot do. We have to do this show now more than ever."

Tess nodded in agreement.

"Girls," Miranda said, looking at us gravely, "this show will do a world of good. Just wait and see. Maybe it will even reach Trent and Chris. You never know, but the important thing is that you try. Try to reach them and everyone."

We took Miranda's advice and ran to find the boys so we could rehearse. We told them about the scenery being sabotaged, and we all set out to rehearse our skit with new energy. We knew what we were doing was right. We went over our skit a couple of times just in the grass behind the stage, and then at 11:00 it was our turn to have the stage for rehearsal. Our skit was short so we had learned all our lines already.

We went through our skit a couple of times, worked on blocking our movements, and even began hamming it up. We were getting into our characters now. It was taking on a life of its own. By the last time we went through it, there were actually a few kids watching us and they were laughing in all the right parts and seemed really into it. It was great!

As we broke for lunch, I warned, "We have to be back here by 1:00, guys. We have dress rehearsal—the big one."

"Let's go to the Corner Cafe," Holden suggested.

I looked at my watch and gave him a look that said "I don't know."

"Come on," Ben pleaded. "We deserve it. Let's go have some fun. And a milk shake. You must have a milk shake before a big performance."

I caved in, and we started off for the cafe. Tess stopped us and said, "I think I…um…I'm going to have lunch with Miranda, if…if you guys don't mind." She looked up at us questioningly. "I have some work to do."

"Well, is everything okay, Tess?" Rebecca asked, voicing all our thoughts.

"Oh, yes, of course," she said with a shy smile. "I just need to talk to her about something." She gave us a quick wink. Then, she was off, trotting back toward the stage.

Now, what is she up to? I wondered.

The rest of us walked over to the cafe, laughing and talking. It was great to be back to normal. We eyed the banner on top of the stage. It looked awesome. I felt like nothing could touch us. Trent and Chris could do whatever they wanted, but I didn't think that it could make a difference. We were doing the right thing today.

We ate our lunch quickly. We could barely wait for 3:00.

"So do you think anyone will show up?" Rebecca asked, shoving some french fries in her mouth.

"My mom is trying to get a phone tree going," I told them. "She's going to call all of the teachers and people in the PTA to get as many people at the show as possible."

"That's awesome," Rebecca said with a smile. "I have to have a large audience for my breakthrough performance," she said, batting her new false eyelashes that she had put on for the show.

"I can't wait to actually get up there and do the skit," said Ben. He was the seasoned professional in the group. Not only had he been the lead in a lot of school productions, but he also worked with the community theater group in the summer. He had even performed on the stage in the square before. "Remember," he told us, "don't get nervous when you look in the crowd. Just remember you're not really you. You're your character."

I was happy to hear the advice. I needed some. I had never been on stage before. Neither had Holden. But I think our excitement overcame our nervousness.

"I'm not nervous about this," Holden announced. "After all, if I can handle eating Ben's mom's chop-suey lasagna, I can get through just about anything." Holden laughed.

"I hear you on that subject, Mr. Cross," Ben agreed. "But let's not start on your mom's tuna casserole. I swear I lost a couple of teeth in that!" We giggled at that one.

We walked hastily back to the stage, quickly scoping out the food booths and carnival games being set up for tonight. As we passed a group of parents chatting on a park bench, we heard them mention our extravaganza. They were talking about coming to see us! Amidst all the activity of the yearly festival in Golden Oaks and with all of the different entertainment they could have been talking about, they were talking about us! We were the talk of the town! Not only that, but the parade route had been changed to end up in the square right around 2:30 so more people would come see us! Rebecca and I exchanged satisfied glances. This was the big time!

As we got closer to the stage, we talked briefly about Trent and Chris. I don't think any of us really wanted to give them any more of our time or concern. We had more important things to think about.

Dress rehearsal went okay, considering we'd had only one day to prepare our performances. There were still some glitches, but we couldn't expect perfection. The overall message was great, and it was going to be a good show.

Rebecca, Tess, and I sat backstage putting the finishing touches on our makeup. We helped some of the other kids make final changes to their skits, while Holden and Ben went to set up the last of the scenery.

At 2:30 I began to get a little nervous. I was pacing back and forth backstage, cracking my knuckles, and my stomach was tied up in knots, partly because of stage fright but mostly because I didn't want Trent and Chris to do anything to mess up our day. Miranda came backstage and asked us to help her with some last-minute things. We were glad to have something to do. As we walked past the curtain, I peeped out and saw that almost all of the folding chairs were filled up already! People were already spreading blankets on the grass behind the folding chairs to watch us! There must have been a hundred people. I pulled

Rebecca and Tess over to the curtain so they could see. "Half the town is here already," Rebecca exclaimed excitedly.

"I know!" I said giggling. "We're going to be famous."

"Oh boy, there are a lot of people out there," said Tess. She hated getting up in front of people.

"Just thank God you decided not to be in the skit, right, Tess?" Rebecca said.

Tess nodded. We hugged each other in excitement. *This is going to be quite an afternoon*, I thought.

We ran around for the next few minutes checking mikes, pinning costumes, and touching up scenery. I felt like we were a part of something really big, and it gave me a great feeling to have been one of the people who started it.

At 3:00 on the dot, we began the show. There would be three acts before ours. We would be the closing act, the finale.

Ben had volunteered to be the emcee. When Miranda gave him his cue, he stepped through the curtain and welcomed everyone. "The Seekers are proud to welcome you to their first annual extravaganza," he began in a booming game-show host voice. The crowd responded with enthusiastic applause. Holden and I just looked at each other and smiled from ear to ear.

The show began with the Explorers singing a jazzed-up version of "Jesus Loves the Little Children," accompanied by a piano, trumpet, and saxophone. They used sign language to go along with it. It looked and sounded beautiful. The song had the theme of accepting others' differences. It was a perfect way to start off our show. When they were finished, the crowd went wild, cheering and clapping. It took Ben a few minutes to quiet them down for the next act. When the Explorers came backstage, they were beaming with pride. I told them what a great job they had done and I meant it.

The next act was put on by a bunch of kids in Seekers. It was called "Different, Who?" The kids had set it up like a late-night talk show. and they had "guests" who were supposed to be famous characters from movies, books, or TV shows. Each character was famous for being different in some way, and most of them had, at one time, been made fun of because they were different. E.T., the alien from the movie, was one of the characters. They also had Jackie Robinson, the first African American major-league baseball player, and President Franklin Roosevelt, who was in a wheelchair. The host asked how it felt to be different, in what ways they felt they were like other people, and whether they felt that being different had any advantages. The guests came up with some creative answers, and the audience loved the skit! I was cheering wildly from backstage.

Next came a skit from some other Seekers kids. It was supposed to be a scene in the Golden Oaks school cafeteria in which some kids wouldn't let nerdy kids sit with them. The scene was very dramatic and ended with the principal breaking up a fist fight between them. At the end of the skit, each actor gave his or her opinion on how the kids in the scene could have handled it differently. It hit home for me and the audience as well. Everyone cheered as the players took their bows.

I had almost forgotten about Chris and Trent and their threat, up until this moment. Now, after that skit, I remembered. I saw them standing in one of the far back rows, doing their usual laughing and horsing around. I figured they would be crazy to try and pull anything with so many people here. This put my fears aside as I heard Ben announcing our skit entitled "Who Knew?"

Ben hurried backstage to get into his costume and makeup while the pianist played to entertain the audience until we were ready. Tess asked us all to hold hands quickly and say a little prayer. We joined hands. Holden was holding my left hand a little too tightly. I figured he was really nervous. I was too. We weren't like Ben and Rebecca. This stage stuff was new to us. My stomach felt like it was doing cartwheels.

"Dear Lord," Tess began, "watch over us as we do this skit, and thank you for how well our show is going."

I asked a silent prayer, "Help us get through to kids like Chris and Trent."

"Amen," we all chimed in.

I looked around at my friends. How funny we all looked! We had on white clown makeup, with black lines making mime faces on each of us. But that was as far as the similarities went. I was wearing a rainbow-colored clown wig and a red nose with humongous shoes and a clown outfit. Holden wore a shaggy blond wig and a shirt with four arms—two were stuffed with socks. Ben was wearing a mask over his mime face. It had crazy green hair and an old man's face. He looked like a mad scientist. Rebecca had wings and looked like a fairy or an angel. She had a long blond wig and a sequined dress. I started to laugh. It made me forget how nervous I was. I could see that everyone else was fighting back the giggles too.

"Not now, guys," Ben said fighting back a chuckle. "We have to get on stage." We nodded. Tess had written a fantastic script and we were on. We ran into position and the curtain pulled back.

The spotlight shone on Rebecca. The rest of us stood perfectly still; we were frozen in our positions like statues, just as we'd planned. The audience fell silent. I glanced out at the throngs of people in the audience. There were parents, kids, grandparents, teachers, friends, but I suddenly wasn't nervous. I took Ben's advice. I wasn't Allie anymore. I was this clown character and I had a job to do.

Rebecca was the first to come to life. She flitted around the stage like a butterfly, her wings fluttering behind her, along with the spotlight. She stopped at Holden. He stood frozen. Rebecca addressed the audience, "He doesn't look like me." Rebecca looked very concerned. Timidly, as if she were scared, she picked up one of Holden's fake arms and let it drop. Holden came to life, yawning as if he had just awakened from a deep sleep. Rebecca jumped back in surprise. "You don't look like me," she repeated very matter-of-factly.

Holden seemed to notice her for the first time. He took a step toward her and sniffed. Looking very curious, Holden walked in a slow circle around Rebecca. He touched one of her wings, sniffed it, and said, "You don't look or smell like me." The audience chuckled lightly, but became quiet again very quickly so they wouldn't miss anything.

Holden and Rebecca began to walk toward Ben, who was still frozen in position. Holden and Rebecca never took their eyes off of one another as they walked, as if they didn't quite trust each other. When they got to Ben, they took turns making exaggerated circles around him, checking out every inch of him. At one point Rebecca and Holden bumped into each other as they were inspecting Ben, and they jumped at the thought of touching each other. They gave one another a look and continued their inspection of Ben. Holden poked at the wrinkles on Ben's mask, and Ben came to life with a start.

"You are not like me," Ben said to Holden and Rebecca. He sounded scared and repulsed.

"You are not like me," Holden repeated to Ben.

"And you are not like me either," Rebecca said. By now, the audience was understanding the message, and it was so quiet I could hear my own breathing. My heart pounded with excitement. I was next.

The three of them looked grumpier than ever as they carefully stepped toward me. They quickly looked me up and down, shook their heads, and then Rebecca purposely stepped on my big clown foot to wake me up. I jumped to life and screamed, "YOU ARE NOTHING LIKE ME!" to all three of them.

A scuffle ensued. We began to fight with each other, throwing fake punches and kicks. All the while, we took turns yelling, "YOU ARE NOT LIKE ME!" After about 30 seconds of this fight, we began to tear off each other's costumes, like it was part of the fight. My multicolored wig lay on the stage, along with Rebecca's wings, and Holden's fake arms.

We dramatically stopped the fighting and looked around at each other as if we were bewildered. Each one of us stripped out of the rest of our costume, and underneath we each had on black pants and a black shirt. We stood, staring at each other—our black outfits with our painted mime faces visible to the crowd. We held our pose for a dramatic moment.

A few people in the audience already understood and began

to clap. Rebecca took a big step toward the audience and said, "We are all the same—underneath." Then, we each took a step forward and said the same thing, each of us in our black outfit and painted face. The crowd exploded in applause, cheering for us. They'd loved it! I had goose bumps up and down my arms. They had gotten the message. *They understand*, I thought. I saw Trent and Chris sitting quietly in the back now. I prayed that they were hearing the thunderous applause, hearing the message. Really hearing it.

The four of us joined hands and took a bow. It was thrilling. The crowd stood up. They actually gave us a standing ovation. I looked at my friends as we took a second bow. They looked exhilarated. We had done it!

Rebecca looked at me and gave me a huge smile. She had tears coming down her face. As we took one last bow, Holden squeezed my hand and winked at me. Ben ran backstage to get Tess. They came back and Ben announced over the microphone that Tess had written the script and put the skit together. The audience applauded loudly for her, and she hid her face in her good hand, but I could see she was smiling. I was so happy for her.

The curtain pulled closed with the audience still cheering loudly. I jumped up and down with excitement. I ran and hugged Rebecca. "We did it," I exclaimed.

"Can you believe they gave us a standing ovation?" she asked. Holden and Ben came over and joined us in a big group hug. We were so excited.

"Wait," I said. "Where's Tess?" I asked, looking around. Just then we heard Miranda's voice over the microphone.

"I thought the show was over after us," Ben said, looking

puzzled. We shrugged and moved closer, trying to hear.

"Thank you, thank you," Miranda was saying, trying to get the audience to quiet down. "What wonderful performances!" The crowd cheered loudly again. "I would like to ask all the participants from today's extravaganza to come on to the stage." She paused, waiting for the curtains to open. All of the actors came scrambling onto the stage. The curtain opened and the audience cheered again. "However," Miranda continued, talking over the noise, "we do have one more treat for you. In light of the fantastic messages that these young people have given us today, we have one more message, one more performer. So if you could, please lend your ear to our next act, our poet, Tess Cole!"

Ben, Rebecca, Holden, and I looked at each other in amazement. Our Tess was going to read one of her poems in public! We stared in disbelief at Tess as she walked up to the podium where Miranda had been standing. Tess looked over at us, gave us a weak, nervous smile and cleared her throat.

"I…um…I wrote a poem for today's show," she said quietly. The audience became perfectly still so they could hear every word. "I never like to…um…talk in front of people, but I thought, well, I thought that today it would be okay. I have one arm that is paralyzed as a result of a car accident, and I thought this poem would go along with the show. So…um…here goes."

Tess began to read her poem and a hush came over the audience. They weren't just listening to Tess, but they were feeling along with Tess, and so was I.

A difference is a musical note,
Sometimes flat,
Sometimes sharp,

But often right on key.
A difference is a grain of sand,
Another color,
Another shape,
Still a part of the sea.
A difference is a flower,
a snowflake, a song,
a child
or maybe even me.

The audience sat silent for a moment and then cheered louder than ever and, for the second time in one day, rose to their feet in honor of something Tess had written. I saw Tess's family in the front row clapping and wiping their eyes. Even G-ma was there. It was touching. *She must have told them*, I thought. I could tell by their faces. I looked around for Trent and Chris, but they were gone.

I looked at Tess, standing at the podium, smiling. My wonderful friend, Tess. This is what she deserved, not angry or threatening notes. This cheering, this acceptance, this is what she deserved. She stepped down from the podium, teary-eyed and laughing, and came running toward all of us. We all hugged her. Rebecca was crying. Holden and Ben looked like they were close to tears. The curtain closed. Miranda said the appropriate thank-yous, and the crowd cheered one last time.

Backstage, we congratulated each other with hugs. My friends and I made sure that we congratulated all of the other kids because their contributions meant just as much and they helped send our message too. We had all banded together to do this great thing. *We really touched people*, I thought. *We'll remember this forever. This is the day that we made a difference.* It was the most wonderful feeling that I had ever felt. At that moment, as I looked at the faces of Holden, Ben, Rebecca, and Tess, I saw them for what they were: the greatest friends that I would ever have.

11

MORE THAN I DREAMED OF

That evening, after I scrubbed off all of my mime make-up, I put on my favorite jean shorts and T-shirt. I was getting ready for the carnival when my mom knocked. "Allie, I just want you to know how proud I am of you," she said with a huge smile.

"Thanks," I said and gave her a big hug. "And thank you for all your help. You really packed the house today."

She looked at me. "You have such a good heart. You really put together a wonderful thing today. You touched people."

I blushed. "It wasn't just me," I said, a little embarrassed. "Everybody helped."

"Yes, but you got the ball rolling. You should be proud of yourself."

"I am," I said truthfully. "I'm very proud."

"How's everything with your friends? You guys all made up now?" she asked, grabbing the hairbrush and putting my hair in a ponytail for me.

"Almost," I said. "I just have to talk to Holden a little bit.

And I will. I'm meeting them all at the carnival in a little bit."

Mom said, "I'm meeting some of the teachers from the high school at the festival, so I'll give you a ride. Come on."

At the carnival, I met up with Ben, Holden, Tess, and Rebecca. We were still riding high from the experience of the afternoon. Kids and parents were congratulating us left and right. Miranda caught up to us when we were waiting in line for cotton candy and popcorn. Her curly red hair shone in the carnival lights.

"Guys," she said with a pleased grin, "I just want you to know that you did God's work today. You really did." We beamed with pride and said our thanks to her for all her help and dedication. We knew that our show never would have happened without her and we told her so.

"Oh! One more thing," Miranda said, as she pulled something from her pocket. She handed it to Tess with a smile. "I'm not supposed to say who it is from," she said, "but they said you would know." We all held our breath as Tess opened the note. After the past few days, we had come to expect the worst.

We looked over her shoulder as Tess read the note out loud. "We're sorry." Tess started to giggle and read the note one more time in disbelief. "We're sorry." And then she read it a third time as if the words were the most wonderful thing she had ever heard. "We're sorry." We all grabbed the note and took turns staring at it. *Can this be real?* I wondered.

"I thought you would be pleased," Miranda said. "They handed me that right after the show today, but I couldn't find you until now. Now you know what an impact you had. Quite an impact." And with that Miranda hugged Tess and went off into the crowd.

"I can't believe this," Tess said, breaking our disbelieving silence. "This is more than I ever dreamed of. An apology. An actual apology."

Rebecca put her arm around Tess and said, "The greatest thing is that you may have stopped those kids from picking on anyone else."

"I think we may have changed those guys," Ben said, looking astonished.

Holden said excitedly, "I have a great idea. Let's invite them to Seekers next week. I'll do it—I know nobody wants to confront them, but I will. I'll just sort of work it into the conversation sometime so that they know they're invited. I mean, I know they'll think it's weird for me to be talking to them, but who cares?"

We all nodded emphatically. *Holden is so...everything*, I thought to myself.

"That sounds like a cool idea," I said. Everything was falling into place.

It was our turn in the snack line, and we all ordered our goodies. Holden and I both wanted cotton candy, so we decided to share. Rebecca got an elephant ear, and Tess and Ben shared some popcorn.

"It's time for the roller coaster," Holden announced. "Let's go, Ben."

"I don't know Holden," Ben said, shaking his head. "I'm kind of chicken when it comes to those things. Besides, Tess wants to go on the Ferris wheel."

"Don't look at me," said Rebecca. "It'll mess up my hair, and there are too many cute guys here."

"I'll go, Holden," I said, loving the way his smile perked up.

We started off toward the roller coaster, sharing the cotton candy. *This is how summer is supposed to be*, I thought. But I knew there was one more thing I had to set right, to take care of. As we sat down in the car for the roller coaster, I kept thinking about how I wanted to explain to Holden that I had thought a lot about what he told me the other day, about how I had been worried about him getting hurt too, about how much I liked it when he held my hand. I wanted to explain that I had just been taken by surprise and that I was confused. I wanted to explain that I had prayed about it and, like everything else, it seemed a lot clearer to me now.

I wanted to tell Holden all of these things and explain myself, but when I looked over at him and saw him looking at me and smiling, I knew I didn't have to. I could see in his bright blue eyes that he understood. He always understood. So, I grabbed Holden's hand and squeezed it. He squeezed back, and neither of us let go.